# Darkness
# Of
# The
# Black

*This is my first short novel.*

# *Darkness Of The Black*

## *Sean McNulty*

DARKNESS OF THE BLACK
Sean McNulty/July 2006


Published by Sean McNulty
Colorado Springs, Colorado


This is a work of fiction. Names and Characters, included places and incidents either are the product of the author's imaginations or are used fictitiously.

Book Design by Roland Ingram

ISBN 978-0-6151-3584-7

*This book is dedicated as thanks for those who help and make this story possible, and for their support of this book.*

*James Sies*
*Roland Ingram*
*Brian Herpel*

*And all of my love to my children*

*Julia McNulty*
*Oliana McNulty*

# Table of Content

# Darkness
# Of
# The
# Black

# Chapter 1

## Childhood

In1974, the mother purchased a black kitten, 6 weeks old. She took care and raised this strong black kitten until she gave childbirth to Kevin on September 13th, 1976. They unintentionally learned that Kevin was deaf. She was panicked about the particular circumstance she was facing. She graciously accepted and raised Kevin until he was 3 years old. His mother generously offered the black cat to him. Kevin was very excited to have the black spoiled cat.

He independently obtained the whole personal responsibility of the black cat. He enjoyed taking care of her, and raised the black cat very well. He named the black cat "Tiger". Kevin was the only one who Tiger could go to for anything. She couldn't go to just anyone, especially strangers. She became very dangerous to anyone she didn't know. Kevin loved this cat very much. He protected her as much as the cat could do for him.

Kevin was 7 years old. He started noticing something obvious about Tiger. Every night, he could see plainly his cat's eye glowing. Tiger stared toward him all the time. He started to feel deep fear of her. He attempted to avoid her by going to his mother's bedroom. All of a sudden, Tiger growled and hissed at him, she definitely gave a scary look, walking in a very slow motion, toward him, jumped on him, and bit his right arm as he tried to defend himself. Kevin shouted. Suddenly, Tiger disappeared. Kevin woke up. Sigh. It was just a bad dream. He went looking for his cat. He successfully found her in the basement and carried her with him to his bedroom, and slept with it.

Five years later, he was 12 years old. Tiger became simple, old, and was not playful anymore. She rested, lying down, as if she was lazy. She came to Kevin as usual. His mother, Terry, started to hate the cat very much. She was eternally hateful at everything. She did a lot of mean and terrible things to the black cat. Kevin always protected his cat every crucial moment, every day, as it seems all the time.

Kevin resided at the school dorm. Seaside School for the Deaf is where he attended from Sunday through Friday. He frequently returned to his home Friday evening, he only spent his time at home for two days. He took trips to school on Sunday, because from where he lived was two or three hours away from the school. He began to have a quite disturbed miserable time at the dorm. He yelled very frequently, massive sweating, shuddering. There was a dorm counselor Kevin trusted with all of his life. His name was Dennis. He was a very superb counselor, impulsive, sweet, honest and decent; he took care of Kevin during the school week.

Terry also trusted him. She expected too much from him for quite a long time. Dennis identified with all the nightmares that Kevin was having. Most of his miseries were about black wild cats, which is just like Tiger. Kevin incessantly talked with Dennis about everything that he dreamed of, he knew all bad or good ones. He started to be concerned about his cat more and more. He was actually concerned very much about her.

Dennis said, "Don't worry. Your mother suggested to me that she will take care of Tiger while you are here at dorm during the school week." Kevin still worried about her nonetheless. That lonely night, Kevin slept. His sweats were coming, so was his shudders. It seems it was a new nightmare being introduced. His nightmare was dreadful, getting worse and getting ugly. He woke up inside his fantasy. He couldn't break out of his nightmare. There were so many black cats running towards him. As he looked at them, they growled and soared on him, assailing him. He yelled as if he saw the shadow. Dennis shook him, trying to wake him up. Finally, he woke up; his body covered with sweat, like condensation. Kevin took a long good shower. After he had the shower, he went to see Dennis and discuss, all night, with him about the nightmares. He had so many unequivocal issues that Dennis didn't have any solutions to them. Dennis began to question why he had this sort of nightmare.

Dennis was working with him to get through all of the nightmares. Some nightmares were successfully deciphered, other subjects remained pending. Kevin said, "Whenever I am with my cat Tiger, no nightmares develop, when we are divided, nightmares consistently come up. Is there anything I can do to restrain it?"

"Hmm. No overall ideas on how to impede or carefully avoid nightmares," Dennis said. They both still were figuring out on that. Kevin was able to control some of the nightmares in the beginning.

One weekend, Kevin returned home from the school bus. He was very excited to see his cat. He steered toward his mother's car. There she was, in her automobile. She appeared very upset by something. It emerged that she broke up with particular problems with her fiancée. Kevin looked like he didn't care about her serious problems. He went to his room to check on his cat. Tiger was sleeping on his stylish bed, looking comfy, and purring loudly. He beamed. He took a diminutive gentle nap with his cat. Everything went pretty well that day. Next day, he woke up; Tiger was currently stood on his chest, looking at his innocent face, hissing. Kevin was frightfully shocked as in a scared simple way. He didn't make any movement, not even his eyes. He tended his eyes, slowly coming straight toward the cat's eye, in a contact manner. Tiger hastily continued her shrieks and hisses. She just all of a sudden disappeared as if she was a ghost. Kevin woke up. He shook very slightly. He thought, 'why does it keep getting worse and worse right now? Is it something I did that was wrong? Or was that a threat signal?

He moved outside, and rode on his favorite bike. He detected other stray cats, most of them were black. It really scared him. They followed everywhere he went on his bike; they hastily ran as fast as he turned his bike pedals. They kept dashing and immediately followed him. He found himself to be too distressed to stop. He kept going and going. He wouldn't be able to stop. Finally, he arrived home; he jumped off the bicycle and sprinted as fast as he could to get in the adoring house. He locked all of the doors and the windows. All these cats still sat around the filled house, sitting, some presently undoubtedly standing, patiently waiting for him to appear. Several strange cat shrieks came toward him when he looked at them. It carried on until the day he had to take off for school.

He was having a massive stronger anxiety attack at the dorm once he completely saw black cats outside the kitchen uncurtained window. His responses were becoming unsophisticated and worse, he dealt a lot of attitude and caused some difficulties with school dorm staff, and some of the teachers. No one barely knew what was actually going on with him at that current time. The only staff who understood what was going on with Kevin was Dennis, his current dorm counselor. He still couldn't resolve how to successfully culminate the nightmares, or his unresolved difficulties.

Dennis went home; and began his constant research on the nightmares through the Internet. He found some interesting informative articles that were similar to Kevin's. He transcribed them, trying to carefully understand all of that. He brought them to school to reveal them to Kevin. It helped them clear up some tiny things. The original interesting article really hardly helped much. They just kept up on research about the discrete incidents. Kevin gave up. He wasn't able to partially understand any of them anymore.

Friday, school closed. He got on his local bus on his way home. He dozed off. He was having some reactions, according to his vision, Tiger passed away in the back yard of his home. Tiger came to him and meowed for help. He woke up. He beamed, it was just some fantasies. He thought that she still was living regardless. If she actually died, her dying could divert him. He arrived home, Tiger was still living.

He had a very good weekend, no nightmares or strange things developed. Tiger was doing very well with him. She slept with her head on his lap or chest all the time as usual. Before he departed for the bus, Tiger surged on his shoulder. She purred. She acted as if she didn't merely want him to leave. He offered her a floury kiss and petted her kindly. He necessarily put her down. He firmly said, "Bye, Tiger. I love you," toward Tiger. Tiger observed him and opened her mouth as she tried to snarl. He believed there was something funny about her, but he certainly didn't want to think about it. He got on the bus, back to school, same as usual.

Monday, school was closed. All students went to the dorm. Dennis came to him and posed him to team up with him to go somewhere special. He took him to the plaza shopping for a few hours. They dined at Tuesday Ruby's. Kevin inquired what was going on. He interrogated Dennis, "Why are you doing all of this for me?"

Dennis said, "Don't worry, nothing special for this, but there is something I want to show you after this. I am convinced that you would want to see it. You will discover it once we arrive there, ok?" Kevin said "ok" as he motioned his head. They went to a place called

"Darkness Cemetery," the secret place where everyone buried their pets. There was a lady who looked like a night witch or something. Dennis introduced Kevin to the lady Nanny, the woman who had a lot of experience with all types of nightmares. She questioned Kevin about his trials. He told her all about it. Nanny was astonished, afraid. She had not seen that for many years. She explicitly made it all clear to him. That he necessarily had to be there for his cat all the time, every moment, every day. It was something that he wasn't able to do. If he did as he was told, the nightmares would cease. Unfortunately, he did not do what he was instructed. Things looked perfectly ugly.

At his age of 14, he already became a delinquent, thorny, involved in all gang things. He still had these nightmares, it never went away, and it always stayed with him, no matter what. Tiger still walked, but with critical needs of her mental health, she became weak. Kevin started to let her go a little bit every day. He recognized it was almost her time to go. He still loved her, she was his absolute best pet he ever had in all his life. He pursued attending his school and lived at the dorm as normal. Dennis was no longer his advisor. He resigned a few years ago for some basis. Kevin was very disappointed at everything, his life. Most of all, he was still being scared and aggravated by his nightmares.

He was lacking, full of bad habits. He smoked reasonable cigarettes, scared others with many horror or unusual stories he could always think of. He didn't have any partner or buddies at all. He was isolated. He protected everything to himself. He was mutually feared and outraged inside his chest, it could not be got rid of. According to his groundless fear, it was black wild cats that he was afraid of, other fears have more nightmares. He now focused on how to get rid of his previous and present nightmares. In some incomprehensible way, he knew how to get rid of them, but something consistently came up wrong before nightmares could be got rid of.

He turned 17, fear and extreme anger still inside him. School was closed for the summer; he had more time to spend his time, looking to find an unconscious way to defeat the nightmares. One bright morning, someone knocked on the front door, and woke Kevin up, his mother was at her work. He opened the front door, looking astounded and delighted. There was Dennis standing in front of the door, delightfully laughing, only saying, "What's up? Long time no see. Come out."

He was kind of happy seeing Dennis, his old dorm counselor. They set out somewhere for entertainment. They talked about many things. Regarding nightmares, Dennis wasn't surprised that he still had those nightmares. Dennis said, "Anyone who has those nightmares, it stays within you, it will never go away. No one is able to eliminate the dreams, dreams are too tough to be defeated. You can't do much about it, but there is one thing you can do about it, is to tightly control the various dreams. That is something you could do."

Kevin laments. He hoped that Dennis told him that a long time ago, so he could be able to do such things with his nightmares. Kevin said, "I still have my cat, Tiger; she is still at my home. Nothing has changed."

According to Dennis, he said, "The reason why I resigned from my job is that I was very furious with the way my job was going." He began to sleep on his job. He was looking for something different, to do something different. He wrote books. He was doing pretty well. He is currently married, and has two kids.

Kevin has complications to deal with, undoubtedly, with help from Dennis. There was some progress with Kevin's drastic situations. He regularly attended some Anger Management Classes, and other classes. He felt he had improved a lot. Students at the school were still harassing him, for many years, nothing new, nothing changed. One night at dorm, one of the students was performing a horror gag, He brought a black cat and instantly put it on Kevin's chest. Kevin was uneasy, sleeping heavily, he couldn't feel anything at that moment. Until he felt something move on his chest, he woke up and looked at it, hellishly shouting loudly, it scared the hell out of him. He realized that it was a strange black cat. He lost his temper toward the student who picked on him. He apparently said to the student, "Do that again, I will break you in two. I really mean it." The student stifled himself and left Kevin alone. It hasn't happened since.

He got home on Friday, earlier that bright morning due to the school being closed for a teacher conference. There was the bad news, his mother Nanny came to him and she looked sad, and kindly told him that his cat Tiger was found dead in the garden a few hours ago. She was having seizures; she finally gave up and let herself go. Kevin immediately became very upset; he had a good cry when he saw the remains of Tiger. He stayed with her for several hours. He hardly let her go. He felt something not right about her sudden death after all. He dug a hole 4 feet deep. He wrapped Tiger gently and softly placed her down inside the gap. He filled up the gap. He had many memories with her. Mostly his memories with Tiger were happy moments. He was in a very deep depression, because of Tiger's mean death. He still thought about his cat. His horrible obsession was increasing, getting worse.

After her death, there were some strange things occurring at his home, when his cruel mother was at work. He suddenly noticed strange things instantly appear and then eventually disappear. He just didn't know what they were. He just put all that aside and paid close attention to what actually was prominent to him. That lonely night, he was sleeping. He woke up inside his dream, he saw Tiger also, and Tiger seemed very furious, hurried fast, like flying to him, treacherously striking, and scratching him roughly, rapidly. There was a lot of blood on his face and back. He woke up sweating. Finally, he had not screamed yet. He inhaled, burdened, wondering why this had occurred again.

He said, "Oh no, not again. Shit." He returned to snooze. There, new things kept coming. He felt as though someone walked towards him very slowly, he felt cold, closer and nearer, he opened his eyes sneakily, identifying the black cat walking towards him, the cat's eyes glowing greenly, Kevin shuddered very lightly. He got closer to the cat, realizing it was Tiger walking on him. He zipped himself under the covering, shuddering hard, and then he stripped the cover that were protecting his head. Tiger fled. He found himself with some scratches on his right wounded arm. He speculated.

A few days later, he necessarily put his nightmares and Tiger's death aside, he started to let it go. He appeared to be getting over it. He recovered normally, as others. He improved a lot at the school, his grades, attitudes, and respects for others. He created some development with some allies. He eventually had a nice girlfriend. He began to hastily forget everything related to Tiger. He just didn't frankly realize that Tiger's immortal soul was still inside him. It could regularly read his senses, emotions, anything he did. The soul didn't frequently reveal itself yet, but will soon.

A few days later, something inside his chest was burning, it felt like saintly fire inside that burned a hole inside the worn body. He was in a lot of pain; he went to see his physician. His wise doctor conveyed, "I don't see anything wrong inside your chest. It turns out to be nothing."

Kevin inquired. What caused this? Was it Tiger's soul that was scorching his chest? Actually, yes it was Tiger, when she was irate or complaining, her filled soul blazed. Kevin said to himself, hollered at himself. He took too many Prevacid, basically nothing worked. "Oh, damn. That hurts," he said. The burns and bitter pain didn't stop its harsh pain. There was nothing that could prevent it.

He went straight home and took a steady long nap. He had quite a few annoying dreams, but nothing leading at an assumed duration. Dennis woke up at midnight, had a perception about Kevin, that he became a cat, like his dead cat. He thought that it was just a stupid vision or nightmare, no big deal. He returned to sleep, he kipped like an infant. He got up at around 5:30 am in the dawn getting ready for work. He smelled something strange from the hall, he opened his room door, he switched on the light, and what he saw scared the shit out of him; many black cats, standing and looking at him, their eyes glowing in a blinking way. Four of them hissed and jumped on him without him realizing that he was being charged. He woke up also, was it an insight or a nightmare? He had to figure it out. He had many unanswered questions. He chose to neglect it. He was ready to leave; and found Kevin asleep on his porch. He looked surprised.

He went to him and woke him up, "What's wrong? Are you fine?" he said.

Kevin said, "Hell, no. I cannot handle the nightmares anymore. I can't stand any of them," He exclaimed. He left with Dennis to head to the school. Dennis told Kevin not to worry too much about it, "Just put it aside for now, and do what you are supposed to at the classes. I will check on you again in the afternoon." Kevin went straight to his first class. Students and the teacher seemed scared of him, but kept cool.

Kevin began to observe objects that others couldn't. He saw 7 black cats walking in the hall by his classroom. He followed them. They all moved outside of school, they walked 2 miles from school, Kevin continued following them. They finally walked into their place, it was a huge cave. It may be a real cave or a spirit cave. It was too early to discover that area. Kevin went to that cave, attempting to illegally enter the cave, but somehow, he peered hard into the cave, the black cat, like a pop, its head with bloods drools, came out of the cave, immediately without Kevin realizing. It scared the hell out of him; he tripped and fell down to the ground. He yelled, stood up and ran as fast as he could. He turned back, countless black cats were running toward his back. They were hissing, growling. He turned and kept rushing to get to school. All of a sudden, the black cats eventually disappeared comparable to what ghosts could do. He panted hard, exuding, as if he was consumed.

"Oh, shit. God. I hope I don't have to revert back there again. Otherwise, I am going to kill myself," he said.

Kevin got a collect call from Dennis, they were just having conversation, nothing related to the nightmares or frightening things he has been through. Dennis posed him to come over to his place. Because Dennis stated to him that he got a lot of backaches. He wasn't able to see his rear through the reflection. Kevin arrived at his place. They talked. "Hey, look at my back and tell me what it looks like, please," said Dennis. Kevin took a look at his back; he was shocked, he told him that he had a lot of scratches and dried blood over his back. It looked like it was scratched by claws. They scattered into each other.

Dennis was off the whole week. Kevin still attended school as usual. He started to query why Dennis hadn't gone back to work. Eventually, he determined to settle a visit to see Dennis. He walked 25 blocks away from school to get to Dennis' place. The front door was released, opened a little wide. He looked concerned, so he entered. He watched for him everywhere, in the cellar and first floors. He took a step to get to the 2nd floor. He found him lying on the ground, two black cats sitting on his back, both cats just whooped and looked at Kevin, in some fashion they stared at Kevin. He dismantled any motion, trying not to produce eye contact with the cats. The black cats walked back and faded away. Kevin ran to Dennis and woke him up, phoned 911. Dennis was in a temporary coma, Kevin was truly upset and outraged within himself.

Kevin reached the age of 19. He graduated his school in 1996. He was very delighted that he was no longer required to attend the high school anymore. He beamed at everyone and said to the school, "Go to Hell!" he laughed. He left the property and never stepped onto the land ever again. He had not seen his trusted friend Dennis for a quite long while. He partied with his partners every weekend, for intoxication. He got drunk every weekend. Because it made his nightmares go away. Actually, it didn't really go away. He just didn't realize, and rejected the nightmares or the dreams. He had gotten worse with his behavioral and emotional problems. He became tough to everyone who tormented him in recent years.

Dennis was still in coma. Nothing changed in him yet. Kevin moved to his modern place. He lived in a bedroom apartment for the beginning. He lit up many candles around inside the apartment, he thought it would avoid the nightmares coming to him. That nighttime, he had a very short dream that he shot up to the window in the lounge, and looked outside of the window. He turned around very slowly, his eye appeared strange, it was not a human eye. Finally, came the whole picture, he became a black cat, his eye moved slow and it shimmered. A scary moment came, Kevin encountered the black cat in the form of human; it turned out to be Kevin himself that would become a black cat. The dream didn't bother him at all during his rest. He snoozed very well, stood up in the daylight as normal.

It sounded like he had finally started letting it go a little bit everyday. Sometimes it became a quiet bothers. He was finding himself able to manage the situation. He went to his old home where he used to live. He walked to the yard and checked to see the burial he made for Tiger. It appeared fine and normal. Nothing unfamiliar appeared at that place at the time. His mother didn't live at that place anymore. She settled in another state. She was presently employed and living a good life. He guessed that everything turned out dull at the place. He thought of it that way at different times, because he couldn't bear the fact that it was not acceptable.

He went inside the home. Strangely, the outside was so hot; climate was at 104, clammy. But inside the house was actually a cold breeze, he felt something was not right about this place. He did not realize that there were a lot kittens and cats inside the house. The cats and kittens that were not black, they lived up on the ground level of the house. He went down to the cellar, completely all of the cats are black who live down there. When he brought a cat that wasn't black down to the basement, it roared and jolted as if it was really scared of black cats, she spiraled off Kevin and rushed back upstairs where it felt safe.

He seemed as if he already got used to the black cats. One of the black cats appeared behind the washer, Kevin turned around to the washer, he gasped. The black cat emerged to be Tiger or she especially looked like her. He was shaking hard, muttering, no tone at all. He appeared very fearful and walked back in a slow manner, shaking continuously. The "Tiger" cat used her tongue to clean around the lips as in "Hmm". It sounded like she was looking forward to assailing Kevin and eating him alive. But nothing happened. Kevin felt a lot of tingling inside both his arms. He glanced at his arms, something inside the arms moved a little. It hurt. He tried to prevent whatever was moving inside both arms.

He left the house in a hurry. He escaped from the house; he was too scared to return to that house. It made his mind go a little crazy. He went to see a counselor, he told the counselor everything. She considered he was delusional and fantasized; she authorized a prescription that could help him relax and intercept the delusions and dreams. Kevin took a chance with the prescribed medicine. He went home and drew a good rest, including with the medicine he obtained. It did improve him to sleep better, but it didn't stop the nightmares. He darned himself, almost to give up. There was lightning flashing or flickering that drew his attention. He acknowledged the phone; it was a doctor calling about Dennis. He was awake from the coma. Kevin went straight away to the hospital. Dennis was a bit confused about where he was. Kevin soothed him down and explained everything that occurred to him. Dennis told him to stay away from any cats, no matter if they are black or colored.

"Just remain the hell away from them. I got into a coma because of them. None of this would have happened to me if you never told me about the nightmares and black cats," he said. Kevin felt badly for putting him through all this. He has been through some rough times now.

Kevin left the hospital, thinking not to disturb Dennis anymore until he figured out all the problems and came face to face with the troubles that he dragged himself into. He resolved very few situations. Most were left unsolved for some reasons. He left the state and moved into a new place. He felt a lot better to reside in Maine. It was the coldest state but better than nothing, he thought.

"Yes! I haven't had nightmares and visions for a long time. I feel a lot better now since I moved here in Maine," Kevin said. Kevin laughed a lot.

A few years later, he was still not married or had any children yet. He looked for a woman who he believed was right for him, but no luck for him. He kept trying so hard to find one. He found out that his mother died of natural causes. He was sad, gloomy in some ways, but he was very happy and delighted she died. He went to the funeral. He visited some of his relatives. Not many of them he got along with. He left instantly after the first day of the funeral. He headed back to his home. He drove 16 hours straight without rest or closing his eyes. He drove 80 mph, which was over the limit speed. Until, he saw the many black cats running along the highway towards his car. He stopped the car in a crazy way, spinning the car. His head bumped into the wheel, bleeding a little.

"Damn. That hurts," said Kevin. He sighed. He took his chance to drive home with the injury. He was afraid to go to hospital and considered a mental illness. He wouldn't take that kind of chance. He got home safe. There was a note and parcel at the front door. He picked them up and went inside his place. He first took a long bath to help him relax. He drank three shots of Vodka. It eased many things off his mind. He stepped out of the tub, he dressed up. He ate whatever was leftover. He felt buzzed. He opened the note, the note says:

*"Dear Kevin,*

*Sorry for all the struggles that I may have caused recently. I left a package for you, it's a surprise one. It will be a valuable use of your time to take a look inside the box. You will enjoy it. I can smell your cat's soul inside of you. I left something inside the parcel that will make you realize what you will see soon enough. Don't let it terrorise you. Think carefully and examine it hard after you see what's inside of the parcel. I will notify you real soon. See you later."*

Kevin felt disordered, he didn't understand any of that. He had no idea what it was all about and who it was from. He risked himself open the parcel. He threw out the parcel and ran away from it. What was in the parcel? There was a black cat's head with open eyes, her eyes were green, glittering, blood leaking down the bottom of the parcel, its jaw opened, showing sharp upper teeth. As it looked at him frankly, in an approach of staring that could startle anyone. The parcel was left on the ground by the entry in the hall. As Kevin went back to his place, the parcel and cat's head disappeared. No blood on the ground. It was clean as usual. His body was shaking and tingling all over even more. It made him go crazy, his fists covering his eyes, he was too scared to reveal his eyes and open them at all in the dark.

His arms started hurting, something inside the arms, pressure, coldest. It produced in him chills. He fell unconscious. Then came the worse nightmare, he woke up inside the dream again, he was laying down on the ground, and he got up. He viewed the cave with the wide hole, he guided himself down there. It was very dark, breezy winds, he kept walking way down. He started to have chest pains, it was getting worse and worse, he removed the lighter from his pocket, and ignited it. He looked at his chest meticulously, there was something inside the body that moved. He felt his chest, it moved very fast as if it was scared of being sensed. He staggered on one knee and bent himself to the ground and something was chewing and chunking on his muscles and skin; it was trying to vacate his chest. As it ripped his skin, he painfully screamed, blood was pouring out of his chest.

He tried to get up to rise. He glanced at his chest again; he could openly see the hole where the chest was. He touched inside the hole, it hurt. He observed the area where he picked himself up from, and directly, the black cat steered toward his legs; she was covered with all the blood and some chunky muscle on her, looking up at Kevin's face. She launched her mouth in a way of beaming. She surged on his shoulder. Kevin recalled the scent of his deceased pet, Tiger. He was tricked into thinking that she was Tiger. It was not Tiger; it was other cats playing with his mind. The black cat spiraled off him and fled, fading. He wasn't able to see the cat. He looked at his chest and tried to restrain the blood, unexpectedly, he noted something new; there was no hole, torn skin or blood on his chest. As it seemed nothing happened to him. He left the cave, strangely thinking about what took place out there in the cave. His idea was to run away directly before he could know. He woke up very weary. And he returned to sleep through the night.

Six months later, he returned to his old home again, paid his stay to appreciate his Tiger in the garden. He perceived something outside of the ground. There were Tiger's arms stuck outside the ground. It looked like she was trying to dig herself out of the ground. It wasn't even decomposed at all. He blew when he saw one of the arms propelling backward. He decided to depart that place. He returned home, reaching his mother in Maine. His mother wanted Kevin to come over and visit for a few nights there. He flew in to Maine, taking only one baggage. He already bought the round trip ticket, just in case he still didn't get along with his mother again.

Kevin hugged his mother, they had a long conservation. Next day, his mother proceeded upstairs and woke him up. She instructed, "You need to get up; I have something to inform you about. Also you need to know the truth." Kevin indicated he was awake. He cleaned himself up. He went to the kitchen to eat breakfast. His mother came, she looked very upset about something. "What's wrong, Mom?" said Kevin.

"Oh, there is something I really have to tell you, because I want you to understand the truth," said Terry.

"What is it?" Kevin asked.

"Oh, God. This is going to be hard for me. Anyway, this is about your pet Tiger's death. The fact is her death was my responsibility," said Terry.

"What do you mean? Your accountability for her death?" said Kevin.

"I executed her with my bare hands, I constricted her and drowned her into the swimming pool, left her to die there," Terry told Kevin.

Kevin was shocked, "How could you do this to me? Why didn't you tell me this before? You a son of bitch," said Kevin. He left untethered. Terry rushed to him and said to him, "I am so sorry. Please forgive me." Kevin would not forgive her at all. Tiger was the best thing that ever happened to him, his whole life. He regarded what his mother had done to him. He never spoke to her again. He walked out of her life for good.

He went to see his friends after he sprang back to his town. Nothing much was going on with his friends. He took a drive with his friends to a bar, he got himself drunk. He lost his temper and couldn't supervise it. He successfully took a long walk to his place. He slept like a cuddly baby.

Dennis's loving wife, Jamie, stopped by Kevin's place. She told him that Dennis did not make it. He died. She cried. She squeezed him, pressed him hard enough for him for him not to be able to breathe. She cried loudly, dropped herself on to the floor, Kevin seized her and lifted her. Kevin asked her to stay over for the night. She took the couch to sleep on. They spoke so much about Dennis and his history that Kevin had with Dennis since the minority. Jamie smiled. She said, "Dennis discussed you, Kevin this, Kevin that, as much as if you were his real son." Kevin sighed quietly. They went to bed, until the morning. Kevin cooked the breakfast, the smell woke Jamie. She just got up in a good mood. She brought many papers that were drawn by Dennis. She asked him what was all that about. Kevin was supremely surprised about the drawn pictures Most of them were drawings of black cats. Some pictures showed bloodshed. She let him keep them all because it upset her so much just thinking about her husband Dennis.

He cleaned up his whole apartment, just keeping himself extraordinarily busy. He was thinking about the death of Tiger. He felt deprived about this. He wondered why Tiger had to be assassinated. There were no reasons to murder her. Her death became his concern now. But he desired to set that aside for a while. He removed the albums of Tiger. He looked through all of them slowly, laughing, distressed, smiling. He had such good significant moments with his pet. There were the best moments that he would never forget. He now had difficulty in some way, roughly letting it go. He turned this into an obsession thing.

Tiger's death started to annoy him, he tried to forget it, but he couldn't. He decided to take it again. There were many new things finally starting to show at his old home. He memorized that he saw Tiger's arms were clinging outside of the ground. It was now gone. He was uninformed on how to answer it. He was taking one move at a time and understanding it. He recovered Tiger in the basement. He gasped, Tiger, herself, a shadow. She sat on top of the freezer. Her eyes were glowing, beautiful, but daunting. Kevin walked toward the cat. Immediately, the cat disappeared as Kevin got closer to it. He was in a bit of turmoil about the disappearance of Tiger. He pondered. He looked around very carefully with discretion. He still had no clues to what Tiger was trying to drag him into. It scared him even more. He gave up and returned to the motel and got his eyes to rest. His nightmare returned. The nightmare was about the death of Tiger. He managed to sleep through the nightmare without major reactions.

# Chapter 2

## Visions of Ghost

That night, Kevin was asleep throughout a bad nightmare, He has no reaction to it. His vision was about Tiger's death. How did she die? Where did she die? What caused all of this? The objective was to help him to trace some suggestions, to gradually solve the unsolved death. It angered him, but he suddenly began to understand what it was all about. "My mother, is she telling me the unpleasant truth about the death of Tiger? Why did she murder the cat?" He was thinking. He was trying to understand the explanations to his modest question. He kept asking himself, "Was she murdered in a madly similar way? What made my mother do such a thing to the cat?"

He retired to his old home again. He was staying there for a handful of days, and trying to constantly understand what actually happened. He walked everywhere inside the house. He could not find anything at the moment. He returned outside in the fiery yard again, to look over everywhere in the area furthermore. He deemed he might have overlooked something. Then he walked past the old large tree, where Tiger was interred. He saw its arm was stuck outside of the ground, moving, bent for a short time then it eventually departed. The stable neighbor approached him and questioned him, what he was doing? Kevin apparently announced, "Nothing. I am just thinking." The neighbor firmly said, "Okay, see you around then. Goodbye." So they left. Kevin started again focusing on something. He felt something pass him inside the wind. He followed the wind flow; it was the right side of the house in the yard. He suddenly noticed there were several large areas of blemished on the grass. He took a closer look at it, it was blood. He touched it with his hand, it was still wet. Was it Tiger's blood or something else? He speculated. Somehow he fell and collapsed, and hit his head on the ground.

There it was again, a recurring dream. Kevin was walking and watching, around the short episode where Tiger's death had occurred. It was almost like an intense vision mixed with the dream. He stood quietly against the house wall at the same area where he found the stain of blood. His mother Terry took Tiger, and put her on the edge of the pool. Tiger sat down, comfortable. She closed her eyes. Terry returned to the pool. She slowly and quietly walked toward the black cat, Tiger, Tiger didn't hear anything. She captured her fast, and tragically drowned her until she had no air. Kevin definitely saw the unvarnished fact. He was gasping at what she did to his cat, Tiger.

He woke up from the blackout. His head had bumped into the ground, it hurt. He had a good cry over his cat's death. He went to an old shed and picked up the adequate material to dig up. He went to Tiger's grave. He dug the shrouded plot. He found her still remains inside the plastic bag. Nothing decayed, as it seemed that she was still in live flesh. He took her out of the plastic bag. He took a strong real hard look at the cat. He looked closer and closer to it. Suddenly, the cat's head moved toward his face and bit him on his nose as if she was laughing at him. Kevin pulled her off his face and threw her away. He left the grisly incident, and his residence. He drove back to his permanent home. He made some calls, make an appropriate reservation with an economy airline. He was attempting to see his cruel mother.

He made a routine visit to see his mother. He came and had an extremely long conservation with his mother about what really happened. He ultimately came face to face with his mother and got a lot of anger out of her. He shouted at her many times, pushing her hard. She fell on the floor. She bellowed and clearly said, "I am so sorry. Don't hurt me."

"Why didn't you tell me this a long time before? What did Tiger do to make you hurt her? She was just a cat. Don't do that again, or you are as good as a dead dog, do you understand?" Kevin said. Terry got herself up and said, "Please leave. I don't want you here any more. You torture me. I was tired of that cat. She disfigured me, all the time for no good reasons. I did my best to treat her well," said Terry.

"Ok, man. You must be stupid. I was the one who was taking care of Tiger, not you. You are anal. I will leave here, I will not visit ever again. I don't want to see your face again. You better not dare to contact me in any way. Do I make myself clear?" said Kevin. Kevin left her home. He made a promise to himself that he would not set his feet on his mother's property again, he never would. He got on his plane. He was on his way back home, again.

He sat on the sofa, and watched a boring movie. He was about to doze off. He fell asleep. He woke up at 2 am in the morning, and decided to dig a new hole for Tiger's body. He went outside and dug a four feet deep hole, he put the body down there. He completed the hole. He sat next to it. "I am sorry for what happened to you. My mother shouldn't have done this to you. I am very angry with her, always will be. I really felt bad that you had to miss all the things that I have had or done in the past. I wish you were there. It would be a lot fun, don't you think? I will never forget you, ever. I will visit, to see you once in a while. I need to go to do what I normally do. Look after yourself. Rest well. See you later, Tiger," said Kevin. He returned to his home.

Dennis's wife came by Kevin's place. She had something for Kevin. Kevin asked "What is it?"

"It's something that Dennis would want you to have," said Jamie. She and Kevin caught up with the news. They shared their pains. They became good friends. Jamie had to leave for her errands. She wanted to go back home before her kids came back from school. Kevin took a short nap in the living room. He went to do some more research on the computer. Kevin looked out of the window and look at the burial plot. The burial was dug again, as if something tried to take its body or Tiger was back alive and trying to get out of the ground. He went down the stairs, and ran to the burial site.

"Her body is gone. How can that be?" said Kevin to himself. He wandered around the building to see if Tiger was around. There was nothing to see. "Damn, where is Tiger?" said Kevin. He went back inside the building on his way to his apartment.

He walked to the kitchen. He was cooking something for his lunch. He was hungry. He ate the whole plate. He chatted on the computer with his friends. He put Tiger's incidents aside for a while. Someone sent Kevin an instant message saying, "Why weren't you there when I died?" from 'unknown'. "What the hell?" said Kevin. Kevin checked on its profile. There was no information on the profile. He typed and sent, "Who are you? What do you mean, I wasn't there when you died? Please explain." He waited for a reply.

"My name is Tiger, a black cat, the one who died by choking and drowning in the pool," said Tiger.

"Oh, shit," Kevin said. "Stop playing with my mind. Tell me who the hell you are. And how did you know about my cat's death?" Kevin typed and sent it. He got the very last reply from Tiger.

"I came out of the ground where you buried me. You took care of me since you were a little boy. You weren't there for me when I needed your help after what happened to me. You are going to regret it." Tiger typed. Kevin turned off the computer right away after this incident.

He went back outside to the burial site, peculiarly, the burial was filled up again, and Tiger's arms were stuck outside the ground. Tiger waved slowly at Kevin. Kevin panicked. He was having a panic attack. He couldn't breathe. He was in shock. He ran all the way the upstairs. He slammed and locked the door. He went back to the windows, looking at the burial site again. Tiger came out of the ground and walked toward him, looking up at the windows where Kevin was at.

"Oh, shit. She saw me, now she is coming after me. Oh, shit," Kevin said. Kevin went to the door, he lay down on the floor and looked through the hole between the floor and door. He saw the shadow of Tiger walking toward the door. She scratched the door, trying to push the door. Kevin ran in backward to the couch. He tried to hide himself on the couch. He still was having a panic attack. He just ignored the panic attack, it did not affect him.

He started to have sights, visions of Tiger's ghost. He went to bed and tried to sleep. He finally fell asleep. He felt something funny, something jumped on his bed from the front edge of the mattress, walking gently and slowly. He kept his eyes closed, he was afraid that something would happen to him if he opened his eyes. It kept walking toward him. Kevin gave up and opened his eyes. A black cat was right on his face. He looked at the black cat, realized that it was Tiger. Tiger looked into Kevin's eyes and glowed; she licked his cheek, and then vanished. He breathed deeply. He was frightened. He went back to sleep.

Kevin sped out and shouted at himself "Damn, I am so late for school." He kept running, and tripped accidentally, he was tripped by a female student.

"Sorry. It was an accident. Are you in any harm? Sorry for my rudeness, by the way, my name is Julianne. What's yours?" said Julianne.

"That is all right, it's Kevin," he smiled. They walked together to get to school, they were given the pass for being late.

They spent some time getting to know each other. They seemed to hit it off with each other. Kevin walked off to his place. He took a quick nap. He had no nightmares or anything that disturbed his nap. He went to his studio, working on an essay for one of his classes, the final essay. He worked on that until around four o'clock in the morning. His essay was done; he printed twenty-three pages of essay.

He failed in his class, regarding his essay, it was dreadful. He was distressed. His teacher gave him one more chance to correct the essay. He had more time to replace all his grammar with one of his programs to help correct the grammar. He seemed lazy with his English, he let the program take care of it. It sounded like cheating. The teacher didn't realize about Kevin's cheats, but gave him the best grade. He smirked. He got away with it. It seemed that no one found out. He made sure that no one would know. He was so witless.

Eventually, over time he became a complex person. Most of the time, he could not handle his problems, he usually ran away from the problem instead of confronting the problems. Kevin was kind of paranoid more often than usual. People thought he was insane, he saw figments of the imagination. People did not understand other people who can see things that they couldn't see. They should not underestimate others' abilities. He was a very special person. He knew more to the truth than anyone did. This may be his reality, not anyone else's. He began to understand his reality, he still denied it in some areas of truth, other areas he already accepted.

His nightmares were distressing. He was able to handle them at this time. He decided to go to see a psychiatrist who had experiences in these fields. He found a psychiatrist named Dr. Duke. He was the best one in these fields. He charged him nearly $160 dollars, hourly.

Kevin explained everything to Dr. Duke, specifically his nightmares and visions of ghosts.

Dr. Duke told him. "Actually, it's normal for these people to have that kind of experience; some people deny having them. You need to start accept the fate or destiny. It's entirely up to you to accept them. There is always a risk."

Kevin thought real hard before taking any kind of action. He would give himself another chance to see if he could get through all of this and get it over with. He assumed that he would able to dispose of these. He was scheduled for the next session in the next two weeks from that day. He felt a bit better, though, there was still a lot of things to learn from.

Kevin was thinking about this girl named Julianne that he had tripped into by accident before. She was the apple of his eyes. He thought he should come see her and ask her to go out with him tonight. He took his chance. He went to Julianne's home and knocked on the front door. Her parents opened the door, asking, "Who are you? Are you here for Julianne?"

"Yes I would like to speak with her shortly, if that is all right with you?" Kevin said. The parents asked him to wait just for a moment; they were going to get her from the backyard. He waited in the porch out front. Julianne patted his back, it scared the hell out of him, and he felt stalked. Kevin asked her if she could go out with him for a little while. Julianne said, "Yes, that would be great." Kevin smiled. Julianne said to pick her up at 7 pm after their dinner was finished.

"I need to go back and finish the chores that were supposedly to be done today," Julianne said.

"Sure, I will see you at 7 o'clock. I will let you go back to what you were doing recently." Kevin said. He left and walked on his way back home. He was delighted about the date tonight. He ate his dinner and went to take a good shower. Indeed, he was already ready for the date. He apparently left at 6:15 pm and took his time walking on the way to Julianne's place. It was getting dark, he felt funny, the air was becoming breezy, he asked other people if they felt the breeze, they denied it, they felt so hot, humid. It was getting colder for Kevin. He just ignored this kind of strange presence. He failed to notice the small, dark creature, nonchalantly prowling its way toward him at a right angle.

Kevin arrived at Julianne's place. Julianne said, "Are you ready to go?"

"Yes, always ready for this," said Kevin. They both started walking and making conversations. It seemed they started to parallel each other in a way or another. Kevin provided an explanation about his nightmares and flashbacks.

"Oh, it sounds really scary, doesn't it?" she said. Then, he took her to his old home, a burial plot of Tiger.

Julianne was freaked as she saw the arms sticking outside the ground. It was a reflex from the movement.

"Hey, why did you bury your cat alive? It moved," she said.

"Actually, it was dead, but an undead one. It has unfinished business," said Kevin. She snickered; thinking it was funny that it was undead. Kevin assumed that she did not understand the whole point. "I will tell you the whole truth when I find it soon," he said.

They went to a diner, and enjoyed eating, and talking. They made some good progress. As if they had already hit it off. They walked for long hours. Kevin took her back home at midnight. Julianne was the apple of his eye. Kevin smiled and said, "Goodnight, I will see you later." She smiled and waved her hand towards him. They split, he walked back his way to his place, he felt the breeze and smelled an odor, it smelled like a rotten, dead body as it was decomposing. He turned his head around back, and saw Tiger following him slowly. His eyes, the pupil were expanded way too large. He tried to deny the fact.

He landed at his home, tried to get some sleep, he couldn't. He was twitchy all night. He was heavy with dread. He took a sleep pill to help himself sleep. He eventually dozed off. In the morning, he awoke, doing what he usually did. He made a call to a psychiatrist about the problems he was having. He had an appointment in the afternoon today. He went to the office, had a long talk with the psychiatrist, Timothy, and she recommended him to take a strong medicine, and gave him a prescription note. He went to the pharmacy, acquired the medicine. He returned to his home. He had a week off ordered by Timothy. The medicine he had was to block the recurring dreams and delusions. He took it as directed, hoping that it would work well on him. Seemingly, the medicine wasn't exactly tremendous; he still had these recurring dreams that night. He was sleepwalking for a few hours. He couldn't remember what had happened at his place. Eventually, he would remember a few things, over time. He was so disappointed with the medicine he took. He took two others pills, which was a high risk, he was such a risk-taker.

Kevin went to bed peacefully, feeling better, he fell asleep, smiling gently. There were no recurring dreams or nightmares. At mid-morning, he felt a slight breeze, he opened his eyes, it was very dark, he couldn't see anything at all in the room. He walked everywhere in his place. He tried to turn on lights, still vague. He looked around and followed where the breeze winds were going. He discovered a dim, shimmering green eye looking towards him. It seemed to keep walking closer toward him, the ever closer. Unexpectedly, he was screaming and shaking, when it jumped and grabbed his shirt on his back.

He called Timothy. Kevin walked to school, pretending nothing happened to him. He assumed that what he has been through wasn't that terrible. He was thinking of a way to get rid of these recurring dreams, he knew he couldn't because he still did not understand what they tried to tell him. Indeed, he ignored it strongly.

Timothy, she thought Kevin was a surrealistic, dreamlike, it wasn't factual, it had not been documented anywhere. She seemed at first, in this case, to think of the possibilities. She researched many cases that were similar to this one. She found some very interesting, and she wanted to work with Kevin. It would be her first time to experience the situation. She had found some tangible evidence according to the nightmares. She gathered all the information, as much as she possibly could.

Along came the horrific dream, one black cat walking slovenly toward Kevin, asleep, and a deadened smell spread into the air. (Cough.) Eyes gaping, the pupils shrinking. The black cat opened its mouth, sharp shiny fangs, growling. He screamed, pulling the blanket over himself, to avoid an assault. Uncovering the blanket as he pushed it away, it stood watching him like a hawk would do to a snake. Its supreme glowing eyes glanced at his eyes, it caused him to feel shaken, shuddery. He tried to close his eyes for a short while. His eyes were open, the black cat continued to stand on his stomach, looking at him as it seemed to appear to. He was appalled, the black cat wasn't going away or fading, none at all, as it seemed alive.

He told that he was required to meet with Timothy, it was her request, urgent. As they discussed it, she realized that the dreams and nightmares weren't always fiction. She considered this was not a fabrication. They both went through it, from the beginning carefully. Flaws were found inside the nightmares, it was something he may have overlooked. He was trying to find all the pieces and put them into a marvelous puzzle.

He became aware of everything that was becoming realistic. Even the nightmares were now a real mode. A black one is motionless at his place. It was unmoving until Kevin was led to believe everything was real, a fact. He accepted what he was about to face. A black one, moving towards him, looking into his eyes, very deep, becoming invisible, fading away, a small shiny smoke went away and entered Kevin's body. It gave him a chill, shuddering, breathing cold air. He gasped, and felt frozen inside his chest.

Knock, knock repeatedly, ring a bell with a flash, Kevin came to the door, "Hey, Julianne. What are you doing here?" Kevin said.

"I think I saw Tiger walking around my place, now I just saw her at the back of your building, I am not sure if it's her," Julianne said.

Kevin scoffed, snickering gently. "Are you positive it's her?" Kevin asked.

"Like I said I am not sure. I think you should see it for yourself," Julianne said.

He walked out of the building, looking around, he lit one of his cigarettes. He didn't realized, a black cat, following behind him. It disappeared then reappeared, repeatedly in turns. He could smell odors; the odors seemed very familiar to him. From his feet, he felt a tingling grow slow over his body. He looked confused.

He spent 3 days in his home, studying and researching the documents that he got from his psychiatrist, Timothy, he carefully read everything, figuring out what really had happened to him. He went on one forum on the Internet, related to the documents he was researching. One instant messenger appeared on his screen, and told him his long belief. He aborted the instant messages that were sent to him.

He caught Timothy online and asked a lot of questions regarding the documents. The story became very interesting for the both of them. They were continuing their research on this thing. They found an excellent, interesting quote from one of the documents that was written by a victim who had a strong experience.

As he read, he interpreted for Timothy on instant messenger. According to the document, the quote spoke about such long believes, it sounded a little feeble. It may be spoken by some crazy people.

A black cat jumped on Kevin's shoulder. It scared the hell out of him. He petted her, scratching gently to comfort her. He finally got used to it a little bit everyday.

"It's very late, you need some rest, please do not forget to take the medicine I prescribed for you," said Timothy.

"Yeah, you are right. I ought to give it a big break just for tonight. Good night," said Kevin.

He took a good shower. He shut his eyes tightly. A few seconds later, he opened his eyes, seeing blood all over him, screaming as much as he could. He closed his eyes all of a sudden, and then opened his eye as in a wink. All the blood had disappeared, as if nothing had happened to him.

He walked to the living room, stopped immediately, looking at the black cat, decomposed, half of its head a skeleton, the other side, flesh. It opened its mouth wide, growling louder, moving very slowly, staring at Kevin. Kevin stayed still, not even moving his eyes or making contact with the black one with his eyes. It limped slightly. Kevin closed his eyes. The black cat vanished without a trace.

He showed up for one of his session with Timothy. As they discussed, planning to set up the video, and audio recorder, and other equipment to identify the presence inside his place. They agreed to do that in the evening. Timothy drove 15 miles to get to Kevin's place. They had everything they needed to set up. They had five video camcorders, 8 audio recorders, and several pieces of equipment. They put these things in each room. Everything was already hooked up.

Timothy was spending her time at his place. She was sleep on the sofa bed. They both were asleep, Timothy felt a shiver, she woke up and turned up the heater control a little higher.

"Whoa. It's too hot here." He was sweating, panting, he went to turn down the controls. Timothy couldn't sleep, she made herself a nice espresso coffee.

"What are you doing up so late? Are you all right?" said Kevin.

"I am so cold, I turned up the heat, but I still am cold," said Timothy.

Kevin was puzzled. He was so hot, while Timothy was cold. It sounds conflicting, unearthly. They talked and talked in the kitchen. "Holy Christ!" she screamed. Kevin turned around all of a sudden and saw a black cat, it sure didn't look like Tiger.

A black cat walked to the counter and jumped to get on it. It sounded starving, growling. He went to get some meat for it. He put it on the counter and walked away a little space from it. They watched it eat. After it was done eating, the black cat walked toward Kevin, sitting down and glaring at him. Its body dissolved into a skeleton quickly.

Timothy freaked after what she saw. She trembled and in a stage of paranoia, she went into the bathroom and locked herself inside. Kevin waited for her to come out of the bathroom a little over 2 hours. He went to the bathroom, banging the door several times. She opened the door, crying, feeling scared. He took her to the living room, trying to comfort her and calm her down a bit.

Again, they were very shivery. Kevin went to one of the video camcorders, the one in the living room by the closet door. He was very astonished by what he saw. He hollered at Timothy. She ran as fast as a rabbit. She joined him watching the screen.

"Oh, shit! Oh no, we are dead."

From the view of the screen, according to the living room, there was nothing but furniture, but in the camcorder screen, there was something showing a visual presence, it was more than a dozen black cats walking, running around, and some of them were staring at the camcorder. All black ones, their eyes became a greenish glow. They disappeared and reappeared, repeatedly in order of steps.

It still didn't stop, black cats frightening them both. Entirely black ones paused, and turned their gruesome heads toward the camcorder, as if they were looking at Kevin and Timothy directly through the camcorder. They unfolded their mouths into a violent look, screeching louder. They were growling at a high pitch, walking toward them through the equipment. Kevin and Timothy walked backward; trying to avoid the camcorder and all other equipment as much as they could.

The black cats had became from flesh to decomposed ones, with all blood and terrible looks. The more they came. walking fast, about to run into the camcorder, strangely, just too many of them came out of the camcorder, it would not stop the flow of the black cats from the camcorder. Black cats attacked Kevin and Timothy in a way of gentle violence. They were running everywhere, growling and glaring at these two. They tried to move away from these black cats. There was a large number of hissing and growling, they were very angry when they were moving. They had no choice but to be still until further.

"Hush! Hush! Do not make any noise, none at all," Kevin said. Timothy nodded as if she understood.

Kevin was attempting to make a very slow move as if in slow motion. Timothy was following his steps. As they moved, the black cats didn't suspect their attempts, as Kevin unlocked the doorknob, it make the sound "click, click". It "woke them up", looking at them rapidly, growling, screeching, running toward them. They had to make a quick move, opening the door, getting out of the room. Kevin locked the door by using his keys. As they running away, the door was banging violently. The door was metal, getting bent, dented.

As they left the building, they were a bit surprised that it was already morning. Kevin sat down on his knees on the ground. He bent and put his hand on the ground, retching over again. He sounded very frightened. Timothy sobbed lightly. They got in one of their cars; driving away as quickly as they could. They agreed to get Julianne with them, because they had a gut feeling that she may be attacked by the black cats.

Julianne heard heavy bangs on the front door. Her parents weren't home, they were out of town for a couple of days.

"Hey, calm down," Julianne said.

"You have to come with us, we have our fears that something bad will happen to you soon," said Kevin.

"What do you mean? Why would something happen to me that may be so bad," said Julianne. Timothy explained everything to her, told her everything to give an understanding. Julianne was like, "Yeah, right," in a nodding way. She was willing to join with them and see what was going on.

They went back to his building; to check out to see if they still were there. As they entered the place, there was nothing to see but a big mess, all the equipment was damaged with bloodstains.

"Whew, what smell is that? What stinks in there? Didn't you keep your place clean?" asked Julianne.

"We don't know what causes these odors, but it could be black cats, the undead, spreading these odors all over my place," said Kevin. Timothy found three tapes that were in good condition, which would give them a chance to prove to Julianne that they were telling the truth.

Julianne believed them, but asked them, "What would you guys do about it? Are you going to stop all of that shit?"

"I am not sure what to say about this, but I think there is one way that we can stop all of that, even to get rid of my damn nightmares I have been having for a few years," Kevin answered.

They called it for a day. Timothy went her way to her home. Kevin joined with his girl on the way to her house, spending the night there. They had a long conservation, he got everything off his chest to her, explained everything, nothing flawed in it. She started to understand the whole picture. She came to him, wanting to make a confession; she admitted that she was falling in love with him. Kevin smiled and said the very same thing. They slowly moved their heads into each other, kissing gently, smoothly. It led them into other things. They made love. After they were done, with what they started, Kevin took her into a Jacuzzi, and it comforted them both together. They slept together on a queen-sized, soft bed. They were so peaceful the whole night.

A few days later, before her parents came back, Julianne want to tell Kevin something special.

"Hey, know what? Guess what?" she said.

"Really? What is it? Tell me, please," said Kevin.

"We are pregnant. Doesn't that surprise you?" she said and smiled. He laughed in excitement. He hugged her gently and he gave a big smile. He said, "I was thinking, about what happened yesterday, we ought to get Timothy, and go back to my building to see if there is anything that can help us find the black cats? What do you say?"

"Sounds good. We need to be cautious and prepared for any new surprises that may approach us," she said.

They meet Timothy at Kevin's place. They all sighed and counted to 3, when they counted to 3, and then they went into his place. Nothing changed there; oddly, there was a blood trail from his place to somewhere. They had no idea where it went.

They spent hours and hours at the place, doing a major cleanup. Timothy collected all the equipment and evidence she possibly could. Everything looked back to normal and on its feet. Kevin was cooking a nice dinner for all three. They talked, laughed, and teased each other. They didn't even want to talk about what had happened. They continued not to mention it. They wanted to have a good dinner and pleasurable evening.

In the morning, they gathered up everything they needed. There was still a blood trail. They intended to follow it. They were discussing their strategies. They insisted on eating breakfast and lunch first before going hunting to where the blood led. They were ready to go. As they were leaving the building, they stood in the front of the back building. Here they go.

# Chapter 3

## Red Crumbs

Here comes the black cat, it was Tiger. She stood right in front of Kevin. She insisted that they carefully follow her. Several times, Tiger would eventually disappear and return in the future. They preferred to follow the blood trail just to be safe. Tiger called a blood trail "Red Crumbs".

The demand was made to Kevin by Tiger. That he had to follow the red crumbs. At that minute, Kevin couldn't understand what she meant by "follow the red crumbs". Tiger said, "You have to figure this out on your own; you are not allowed to ask anyone for aid on this one. This verifies you have the courage." She suddenly vanished into the air and was flown by the wind.

Kevin could not listen carefully to what Tiger told him. Everyone sighed.

"Is everyone ready?" Kevin asked. They all looked skittish, and followed the red crumbs cautiously without any errors. Timothy knee knelt down, and sniffed the red crumbs. "Whew, strong odors. All right, it's real blood," said Timothy. They walked instead of taking the car, because they were scared that it would forget it, or shatter it. They felt it was very wise to follow; it would lead them right to it without any mistakes.

At the 8 miles they walked, the red crumbs continued carrying on. They approached something that was very interesting, a new discovery, there were three trail of bloods, it cleverly looked like a hayfork.

"Strange, why are there three? Which one will lead us to where you are wanted to be?" Julianne asked, sighing.

"That is a good question. Do I have answers to the problem? No, I do not have one. Anyone has an idea?" Kevin said. No one was prepared to acknowledge that riddle. "It was just a trial for me," he said.

They remained there for a little while, so Kevin could resolve what would be the best answer to its riddle.

Timothy called Kevin, "I heard something like a screech. I am not convinced."

"Huh? Is there something here right now?" Kevin said. On the spur of the minute, a black cat arose on the middle of the three blood trails. Then another one appeared at the right of the hayfork. Again, a black one, alike, unexpectedly appeared on the left of the hayfork. From the look of them, it was a starting riddle. All these three were alike, resembling Tiger. The left one had solid black eyes. The right one had green eyes. The middle one revealed greenish glowing eyes.

Kevin tried to think real hard. He looked at each of these trails with black cats, carefully. It rang a bell, Tiger had glimmery greenish eyes in the dark. He chose the middle trail. He sensed he did answer exactly. He stated that these two people should follow him, behind him. He had to be in front of these people. It led them into Rittenpark Woods. It was the area that was full of woods, large creeks, many routes of walking and bike trails. The survey of Rittenpark had refreshed Kevin's memories. When he was a young boy, he consistently went there playing, walking, into the creek, making a fool of himself. He grinned when he thought of that memory.

They walked and walked approximately 23 miles inside the woods, by the hydroelectric creek.

"I need a big break. That is quite a long journey; it's more than I would predict. When are we going to recover from it?" Timothy said, panting.

"All right, we are going to take an hour or two for a break. Let's eat, we all are starving, aren't we?" said Kevin.

"Whew. I wish to understand, why you are the one they chose? Why you? Help me understand," she said.

"Um, I had this black cat called Tiger, as you met back at the building, the one standing right front of me, I had her since I was born, my mother bought it two years before I was brought to this earth. She died a few years ago in a violent way. That is when the nightmares started. I am starting to be able to observe the truth. As I found out, my mother murdered her by drowning her in the swimming pool. Get what I am saying?" said Kevin.

"Let's go walk a couple more miles. Then we will set up camp and have a fire. We'll rest for the night," he said. They went another 9 miles. During the 9 miles, all these three didn't even notice anything strange. Kevin stopped himself, he felt the very cold air, it made him shiver from the back. He moved around and saw five black ones, slowly walking towards him, and the other people.

"What is wrong? Are you all right?" Julianne asked.

"Hey you two better look what is behind you now," Kevin said. As they turned around, she screamed and dashed as fast as she could. Timothy was shaking, about to have a panic attack. She forgot, she didn't have anything to prevent his panic attack. As Julianne kept running and screaming, it vexed these black cats. It make them very aggravated, and they chased her, they jumped over Kevin and Timothy, it was scary moment as they jumped over them, their bodies suddenly became disintegrated, into skeletons, blood covering them all.

(Clangs) (Screech) Timothy stopped, "Be quiet. I heard something, it's getting closer," she said. The sounds were getting awful closer.

"Run for your life, NOW." Kevin and Timothy ran without looking back. They were searching for Julianne. They split, because they had no choice. Kevin dared to look back, more than a dozen black cats ran, screaming, and hissing. They all three were so completely lost. They had no idea where they were but only Kevin knew what to do. He walked quietly to be sure that no one else was around him. He was very furious by what happened recently. He took six pills of Alert, a medicine to keep him awake. It actually helped him. He found the trail; he set up the two tents, and started up the fire. He hoped the fire would guide them to find him. It had already turned to night.

At the darkest point of night, he was dreaming, he didn't even wink once. He looked at the fire very deeply. A black cat jumped out of the fire, grabbing his face, clawing, and attacking him. He shouted, Timothy shook him to wake him up. Unexpectedly "What happened to you? You look like you had a nightmare. Scratches all over your face, bleeding," said Timothy.

"Yeah, a black cat attacked me and scratched my face. Shit," Kevin said. He had a small cloth, cleaning out his face easily. "Have you seen Julianne? I haven't," said Timothy.

"No, I haven't found her yet. I have no idea where to start," said Kevin. "Let's call in tonight, we need to get some good rest for tomorrow," he said.

In the very early morning, they packed everything, and poured the water over the fireplace to kill the fire.

"It seems that we will have to walk a lot more of miles, it sure is a long trail, I assume," Kevin said.

"Yeah, I can see that. I do not have any problems with that," Timothy said. They set their feet and carried on without any breaks for 20 miles.

"Whoa, this forest is way too large, isn't it?" said Kevin.

"That would definitely be a long way. My feet are killing me, I need a big break," Timothy said.

While they were both walking more miles, there was Julianne hiding in a large hole of a tree. All dirty, muddy, smells covering her. She was very frightened. Her pupils were expanded more than normal. She was shivering, peeking through small tree holes to see if any black cats were around her, yet there were none. She crawled out of the large tree hole. She walked deliberately. She had tired herself. She was weakening, worn out, very drained. She tried to run as much as she could. She was searching for Kevin and Timothy. She hardly gave up finding these two.

She only had a little food left , no water or any beverages. She was starving to death. She looked for the trail that she got herself off from. She cried, thinking many things about her and her lover Kevin. She turned around; quickly saw a black cat appear out of nowhere. Then there were more, dozens appearing instantly. She screamed hard, truly louder, but strangely, no one was able to hear her screams. She lost her mind, and ran like a mouse. She tried not to look back while running, eventually, she made a mistake by looking back, a black cat successfully jumped and grabbed her back, clawing her down. There was blood flowing on her back. She fell down several time due to nausea, and was about to black out. She acted like a drunk, became unbalanced, fell down the creek, into a heavy faint. She was so completely lost in the Rittenpark Woods. She was being left there. Many of the black cats were sitting, acting guardians of her body.

Kevin and Timothy, they walked unsuspecting and not realizing, there were several black cats walking behind them. Kevin was tripped by an unnoticed rock, he fell down, and saw some black decomposed cats, with blood covering them. Kevin and Timothy panicked terrible, and ran rapidly. They both got split up, hiding wherever they could find. Timothy found a piece of cloth, which he believed belonged to Julianne. He made a tough decision, to search for her, he found the shoeprints, he insisted on following it. Kevin hid in a very old rotten small cabin, staying there for an hour or less.

According to Timothy, he found some more shoeprints; he hoped it would be Julianne. "JULIANNE, JULIANNE, WHERE ARE YOU?" he screamed. He knew she was deaf, but he was willing to take the chance just in case. He had a good cry, sniffing lightly, and noticed there was a blood spot, he kept taking steps forward and found more blood spots. He kept looking for more, he felt he could find her closer than he thought. He panted, worn out, still tough, he ran lightly, and saw two legs on top of the ground and creek.

"Oh shit. That has to be Julianne," he said. "Oh, my god," he put his hand under her head softly, shaking her a little, to get her to wake up, "Are you all right? You bumped your head, were you blacked out?" he asked.

"Black cats attacked me from my back, felt like I was stabbed. Yeah, I fainted," she said.

He yanked her out of the creek, picked her up, and carried her on his back. "All right, we got to find Kevin before anything happens to him," he said. They tracked the trail back to where they were supposed to be. They got back on the trail; he gave her some clear liquid. She drank too fast, she wanted more water. He put her down on the ground, cleaned off her face, and tried to fix her back with all the cuts. She gasped, screaming painfully, "Go easy on these, please. I am so scared; it feels like I am having delusions or hallucinations. It seems real," Julianne said.

"I know what you mean; by the way, it's not delusions or hallucinations. It's very real. I am sorry that Kevin had to bring you into this. I truly am sorry," he said.

"I am sure he did not mean it. He might think that I would be helpful in some way." They both set their butts on the ground; and started up the fire to keep them warm. They stayed up all night; waiting for a signal from Kevin. They hoped he would find them before the fire faded away. They both stayed in that area for three days, still no luck about Kevin.

Kevin hid in a deep hole of the ground for 3 days in a row, he hadn't seen any light. He got badly cut on his leg; he had to use one of his clothes to tie it off to pressurize the bleed. He climbed out the hole. He sighed. It was such a difficulty for him to walk very much. He walked slowly and rested quite a bit. He saw the smoke up in the air; he assumed that it would be Timothy. A black cat came to him by smelling his blood from his leg, he licked the cut, the entire, cut was suddenly healed, and the scar was gone. It disappeared without any warning or saying anything. He smiled and chuckled, got up and walked to the place where smoke was. It was a firing place, but there was no one there. He became concerned about them. He kept thinking positive, but sighed again. He kept walking toward where he was supposed to go.

He noticed there were numerous paw prints on the trail, "Damn. Where could they be? They ought to be all right after all," He said to himself. He had no choice but to keep walking and searching for them. He unpacked several things to reduce the weights, the faster he walked. He saw a broken sign on the ground, he picked it up, and he read the sign that said, "Do not enter or it's your death." It scared him a bit, it made him wonder about something. As it seemed, refreshing his memories, back in his younger age, he was 13 years old, he walked past the very same sign, he returned without any harm. Apparently, he remembered he met one of the black cats, inhabitant or inhumane. Its look had been forgotten. He felt that it was a clue that could take him into the past. He was not aware of it.

He sighed several times, taking a deep breath, and ready to walk in. He walked past the sign, everywhere in the wood looked a bit burned, dead, and rotten. He took a long walk; he sensed that the place was getting closer and closer. He smelled something like perfume, it reminded him of Julianne, his lover. He knew she was somewhere closer, he became a little more full of excitement and exhaustion.

Kevin was running and found the red crumbs, he got on it and followed it with caution. Julianne felt washed-out by walking. She became very stubborn, more than anyone had seen.

"Take it easy. You were pushing yourself pretty hard. Calm down, please," Timothy said.

"Don't say another word, NOT A WORD," she spoke to him angrily. He kept his mouth to himself; attempting to get her to cool down. "I am so afraid, I would feel a lot safer if Kevin was with or around me," she said, sobbing loudly. Timothy hugged her to comfort her ,and held her tightly, he told her "Try not to cry, it will not help us at all."

Quietly in the evening, about sunset, Timothy and Julianne were totally worn out, both panting, and dropped themselves down to the ground. Then came the unrealized event, they dozed off all of a sudden, all the black cats appeared, walking around them, glaring, and stalking them all the night.

Kevin was walking throughout woods, making guttural sighs, pretending that he didn't see anything but woods. There was numerous black cats sitting and walking, lying down on the trees, in the branches up high. He knew they were around him, he tried not to let that bother him in any way.

Kevin ran like jogging, calm, relaxed. He tried not to think of anything related to the black cats. It helped so little. He smiled, thinking about Julianne. It made him laugh for some unknown reason. He did some walking for a few more miles, giving himself a big break, setting up his cottage, fireplace. He sat outside, looking at the sky, counting the stars.

Timothy woke up and could smell burning. "Holy shit, it's the smell of fire. Where could that be?" he said to himself. He shook Julianne a little too intensely. Finally, she woke up. "What? I am too tired. Let me go back to sleep for a while, I will feel a lot better," she said.

"Hey, I smell the fire, there is something? That is possible it's Kevin," he said. They walked and followed the signal of smoke.

"I am not feeling well. I am feeling a heavy nausea," she said.

"Hang on. Let's get going to the fire. Then we will see what to do from there," he said. They were getting close to the fire. He saw Kevin standing by the fireplace.

"Jesus Christ, he's sleepwalking again," he said. They ran in a hurry. Finally, they got there, and Julianne slapped Kevin's face pretty rough. He could not wake; the slapping was kept up repeatedly in turn on both sides.

He was sleepwalking, petting a black cat in his arms, they both could not see it, only Kevin had the ability. He was puzzled while the black cat dissolved slowly, into a skeleton, he screamed in panic. He woke up from sleepwalking, "What happened? Did you see the black cat? I was holding her in my arms," he said.

"No, I didn't see anything in your arms, you were acting like you were holding something ghostly in your arms. Hey, you all right?" they both said. They lay down the ground to rest; Timothy wasn't able to rest after all. Julianne fell asleep. Kevin just closed his eye, but refused to sleep.

In the very early morning, Kevin woke everyone up. He said, "It's closer, just a few miles away. We don't need to pack anything, except foods and drinks."

"I feel a little better now," she said.

"Bravo," Timothy said.

They continued their walk down the red crumbs. During the fourteen miles, there were many events, strange presences, it was so many, countless. The air become full with strong odors, the woods looked creepier, and there were unrecognizable noises. There was a small pet cemetery, covered in fog on the lower part, of the ground. There were several crosses of woods, held in the ground, there were five tombstones, with messages on them. There was some damage on them, it was so unreadable. They wrote down everything, just exactly as the tombstones' messages said. They got to figuring out the blanks to be filled in. They all spent all afternoon there. Julianne walked and looked around, she approached a stone house, it looked creepy. There were plants all over the stone house; the windows were firm, undamaged.

She went to get Kevin, and told him about this stone house. It interested him to visit that house. Timothy wanted to join, to learn more about the pet cemetery, such a very motivated person, a risk-taker. As he opened the door of the stone house, gusts of frizzy dusts blew out of the door, "Whew, that's the worst stink than anything I have smelled before," Timothy said, Coughing and sniffing. As they got into the house, "Wow, my god, look at this place," said Julianne.

"Yeah, I think that is the way it looks in every stone house, I do not know for sure. This is first time for me to break and enter this house," Kevin said.

There was only one stair, it was so dark, no one was able to see. "Whoop",) the firelight on both side of the wall between the stairs, lit itself, it was getting brighter, enough for them to see where they were going.

"It seems they already knew we are here in this creepy place," Julianne said. It took three hours of walking down deep in the catacombs. As they walked deeper, they could see many skeletons of cats lying down in the holes of the wall. "Holy shit, this stone house is the black cat's home, isn't it?" Timothy said.

There was a stone door down the stairs, Kevin went to the door, trying to get it open, and he could not. Kevin walked backward, waiting for signals, as he suspected. They stood for about fifteen minutes; no one was opening the stone door. There was a small blue fire in the center of the door, as it grew bigger, the bluer it became, it is called 'Blue Fire'. It's not harmful fire; Kevin put his hand over it, there was a response to it. The door opened itself. Gusts of wind blew out of the door with sand, webs, it was strong enough to push the three off.

"Whoa. The door is opened. Let's go inside before it closes and seals it again." They rushed into the next room. "Oh, my god. There are dozens of skeletons of cats everywhere. Some are still decomposing as it seems," said Kevin. There was a sound that was so loud, it scared the hell out of them, it was whoosh, several skeletons and decomposed cats arose, there was growling, screeching all over. All the cats formed a straight line, standing and looking toward the three people.

"They are looking at us, aren't they?" said Kevin.

"Let's find out. We will know who they are actually looking at, or want to attach with," said Timothy. Kevin first took a few steps; Julianne and Timothy didn't take a step. They were not moving. All the cats made their move, heading towards Kevin, and following him as he moved toward them. "They want you, not us. Let's not stall them, do what they ask you to," Timothy said.

"All right, I will do my best not to get clawed or killed," said Kevin.

"Hey, be careful. Don't do anything stupid," said Julianne, and kissed him.

"Here I am, let's do this. It shouldn't be hard," he said sighing. He took a step toward them slowly. The cats followed his steps like a king. He turned his head around and looked at them. "Are they worshipping me? Damn," he said to himself. He stopped walking, he found himself in a room with a big coffin in the center.

He froze, he was shocked like, "Oh shit". There was seven black cats standing in the front of the coffin, they came to him, turned around and walked back to where they came from, Kevin followed them, and he was right in front of the coffin. There was a small sign on the coffin that said as shown; "For those who opens the coffin, shall acquire a key to the Cave of Cat's Eye. Once you enter, there shall be no turning back." He pushed the heavier concrete top of the coffin, grunting, panting, and sighing, successfully opened it wide.

He sees a shiny brass key right in the coffin with only one cat skeleton holding it. He shook the key to get it out of its skeleton. He picked it up and smiled. "Now I have it, what next? I got to go get the others," he said. He turned around. All the cats had already disappeared without any messages, clues, and hints, nothing at all. He walked quickly back to where the other two were.

"Hey, are you all right? What happened in there?" Timothy asked.

"Yes, I am fine. They guided me to find the key to Cave of Cat's Eye, that is what I was told, to go there now. We are going there right now," Kevin said. "Let's get out of here before they bite our asses to dust," he said, laughing lightly. They walked and did some running, as fast as they could before the place collapsed. Timothy tripped on something and cracked his right leg, Kevin pulled him up and carried him as much as possible. They kept running, a long way , it took a few hours for them to get to the outside. Finally, as they got out of the stone house, it collapsed to the ground, it sealed itself, there was no way to go back there.

"It collapsed. Oh, no. We might need to go back there just in case. Now, we are stuck," said Julianne.

"There is no turning back, like the sign on the coffin stated," Kevin said.

"Let's spend a night here, let's have a fire, we are too tired to take another walk," Timothy said.

"I am so starving, you guys? I got some marshmallows here," said Kevin. Everyone laughed. They rested their eyes until the morning. The fire was still there. There was no trouble appearing during the night.

As morning grew, a black cat stood, and waited for them to wake up. This black cat looked a half skeleton, half decomposed. It looked very fierce and horrific. Julianne opened her eye, noticed there was a black cat standing by her face, she screamed, crawling away from it, and she woke the others. "Whoa. What the hell is it doing here, looking at us?" Kevin said. "Here we go, get back to the red crumbs, and follow it."

These three people walked 32 miles more, which they hoped that would be all. "Why do we all have to do all this walking? We should have driven the car. It would be quicker, wouldn't it?" Timothy said. The sign on a large old tree, it said "Two miles to the Cave of the Cat's Eye.

"Finally, we are getting there. Thank God," Julianne said.

"Whew, yeah, it is not far. We can do it, can't we?" Kevin said.

Another two miles they walked, as they approached the big cave. "Ahh, we made it without a scratch," Timothy said. Everyone laughed, and shouted, "Damn, we made it."

"Let's rest again, just for another few hours, if that is all right with all of you?" Kevin said. They agreed with Kevin's suggestion.

As soon as they gained their energy for another chaos, they got up, and left all their stuff except Timothy's video camcorder. They walked toward the cave. They all three stood right in front of the Cave of Cat's Eye. They sighed, "Are we all ready? This is where the truth lies," said Kevin. They looked at the cave again, smiling. They sounded as if they were not afraid of anything or were happy they found it. Along came the scary chills.

# Chapter 4

## Cave of the Cat's Eye

As they stand in front of the Cave of the Cat's Eye, Kevin giggled and Timothy laughed moderately. Julianne was nervous, walking in paces back and forth . She was getting on their nerves rapidly. Timothy nabbed her and stopped her from pacing. "What are you doing? You are getting on our nerves, we can't stand it," Timothy said.

"I am anxious as much as you two are. I was wondering what would happen to us once we go in the cave. I do have the right to be nervous, don't I?" she said.

They all sighed. Kevin was the first one to walk into the cave. Julianne was second to step inside shakily. Timothy was the last to enter the cave without any reply. Strong smelly stenches appeared all the way down in the cave. They all couldn't stand the smell, they gagged, nearly retching. Strangely, Blue fire suddenly lit itself on the wall of the hall as they walked forward.

"Why are all the fires blue? What's so special about that? I assume fire is generally orange and red?" said Timothy.

"Well, it's called Blue Fire. Like I said, it's not hazardous," said Kevin.

"Let's just follow the blue fire, otherwise there could be something bad happen to us" Timothy said. As they walked at normal speed, stopping in the cave to fathom out where to go next. All of sudden, the blue fires vanished.

"What is going on? Why have the blue fires perished?" said Julianne.

"No idea, I am not sure. Let's calm down, and see what is turning out," said Timothy.

They walked back to each other and stuck together, watching and anticipating for the upcoming event. First glowing eyes opened and blinked steadily. Then others fell upon as they blinked their eyes, a greenish glow. They all were watching these three people, not making any charge or anything, just watching them quietly. Blue fires lit up again.

"Holy shit," Kevin said, so many black cats are gathering in the middle of it. Black cats similarly sat up and looked at them, like a spotlight at them, and make a spacious pathway for them to walk through. It was nice of them to form one for them.

Julianne was walking at the front of the line. Kevin and Timothy were behind her as she walked through the path. "I believe it is better if I go walk in front of you two instead of you. It is for your own security," said Kevin. Julianne and Timothy had no objections. Their camcorder was still powered and recording the outcome.

"Please do not make any noise; we perhaps made them feel that we were attacking them. Let's exercise caution, got it?" Julianne said. They acknowledged her that they got it.

The blue fires continued lighting up as normal. The path had led them to the next dungeon. The dungeon was becoming more clear, in plain view. There was not much of an event at the time. They kept hiking and took several breaks to rest.

"It was not as bad as we had supposed, was it?" said Timothy.

"No. Nothing much to view in this dungeon, but I understand that there will be some events upcoming," said Kevin. Julianne panted, she was very tired. She looked deteriorated, she had been through some rough times as these two had.

A breeze blew through the dungeon, they were so cool. They felt as if they had gone to the North Pole. Kevin kept rubbing himself by his arms to remain warm while walking. They walked slower and slower, caused by the frigid wind.

"Hurry, I cannot stand this damn cold," Timothy said.

"Hey, there's an easier way out, I am sure of it. Let's not give up," Kevin said. They had trouble keeping up walking, but they had not given up yet. They ultimately found a way out, an irrevocably, warm area.

Julianne fell gently; she seemed very pale, as though broken. Kevin picked her up and carried her to somewhere that was easy for her to rest. They sought a place; it took them a mile to find one.

"Timothy, I have thought a lot about this one, it's very difficult for me to conclude. I suppose it's better if I go alone from here now. You stay with Julianne until I recoup, hopefully," said Kevin.

"Are you sure? You don't know what will occur to you if you go alone. You might not return after you explore that place, I am terrified," Timothy said.

"At least, I am on my own now. I will be outstanding, I will be back, I promise," Kevin said. He walked away from his pals. Timothy was very concerned about him. He focused on Julianne right now. He tipped some water into her dry mouth. Kevin moved into a very large empty dungeon, with seven "Blue Fires". He walked into the core of the dungeon room. There was a shining bright blue light orb flying around him, he turned his head in many angles to follow the blue orb. It expanded the light even brighter. Now, he could see clearly in the room, it was full of black cats staring at him. It didn't even make him anxious, it sounded like he was already used to their actions.

"Why am I the chosen one? Why me?" said Kevin. He suddenly fainted on the ground.

Julianne blinked her eyes a few times. Timothy commented to her, "You all right? You had us going, just because of this," they both laughed.

"Where is Kevin? What happened to me?" Julianne asked.

"He went to find the place himself alone now. We'll wait for his return, I specifically have to honor his requests otherwise I'd retrieve him," said Timothy.

Kevin remained in a faint, his body frozen, not moving at all.

Timothy saw something come toward him and Julianne. He focused his eyes to be able to see what it was. There was an unfriendly large black cat running toward them, "Go now, and rush now, before it gets you. Go now," said Timothy. Julianne also ran and didn't even look back. Timothy was blitzed by a black cat, the one with red glowing eyes. He was grazed, not bad, but scratches and bleeding lightly. She sped up, she lost herself into a dungeon maze, and it confused her. "KEVIN, KEVIN, KEVIN," she shouted.

Kevin was still lying on the ground, three dozen black cats were around him, they walked around him. They started to sprint lightly, then roughly, jumping up into the air, becoming dissolved ones, and breaking into Kevin's body as if they were ghosts. They didn't stop jumping into his body. It made his body shake and bounce unstoppably.

A bleed appeared from his mouth, light not heavy. He opened his eyes very slowly, there was something new about his eyes. His eyes were all black, he closed his eyes instantly. He was startled in anguish. He screamed in excruciating pain, panting.

Timothy sat up and leaned his back into the wall. He was panting heavily due to bleeding, he was wobbly. He ripped one of his shirts he was wearing and wrapped it firmly, to manage the rate of bleeding. "Shit, I got to go get Kevin before it is too late," he said. He grunted as he tried to get up off the ground.

Julianne found a dungeon with all items like foods, shelter, among other things. She breathed and laughed. She rushed to get the blankets she could recover, bundled herself into a warm position. She tried to compose herself, without any fuss, all that shouting as only a little girl could. She began searching around to recover the foods she could, the attractive dirty girl was starving. She recovered some water and swallowed it all. She was quite dehydrated. She laughed like she would burst.

Kevin finally woke up from the blackout, screaming loudly enough to produce an echo. His body wasn't as it was before; he felt a lot of suspicious changes and more effective inside the body. He was not able to handle this at the moment. "Damn all these pains. What do I do to get rid of these pains?" he said to himself. A smoke in front of him, formed into Tiger, his decreased pet. Tiger walked around rubbing his legs, to relieve him and it. His eyes became a glowing shimmer.

Kevin lost all of his energy which was taken by the black cats. It was completely gone. Tiger walked away from him; he intended to follow it anywhere it went. He walked weakly and limply. Tiger was generous enough to wait for him to catch up with it. Its eye became glowing, into a very dark area; Kevin couldn't see anything without its glowing eyes. He could see where he was going. He continued following it as he was urged to.

Timothy tracked down a dungeon where Kevin went in; he didn't see anything except black acts with greenish eyes glaring at him. He was rattled a little; he was threatened by these, that they might attack him further like last time. He concluded his search and kept taking steps toward the next one. He smelled combustion and could see a blue flame in the next dungeon area. He was puzzled and he aimed to enter the room, all of sudden, he was forbidden, there was some sort of barrier right at the entrance.

He felt something like a physical presence right in the room he was standing in. He shut his eyes for few seconds then reopened them, he saw three red glowing eyed-black cats. They were sitting right in front of him, they opened their mouth, as in an attempt to growl or screech at him.

"You fucking little black cats. You think you can scare the shit out of me? Show me," he said. He made himself into a strong warrior, attacking the first ones on the right of the three. He picked it up, it tried to get itself off his hand, by shaking and making sudden moves. It missed; Timothy got an opportunity to terminate it, wrecking its skull and splitting it. He in succeeded liquidating all of these three. The barrier was opening by itself, "See? Don't fuck with the wrong person. You all go to hell," he said. He entered the room, inspecting it.

Tiger remained walking; the coming event would take place in the next room. Kevin flopped down, he felt so weak, so sleepy, he allowed himself to sleep for a while. He dropped off on the ground of the dungeon. He was exhausted, gasped for air.

Julianne happened to find a matchbox, she sighed. She lit one of the matches, to be able to see where she was. Once she lit the match, she looked around and screamed. There were dozen of piles of cat skeletons and even some human ones. She was terrified by what she seeing. She ran hastily out of that dungeon room. She screamed without anyone around, "KEVIN, TIMOTHY, WHERE ARE YOU?" she sobbed.

Timothy limped still, looking for Julianne, he was about to break the promise he made with Kevin. He limped and fell repeatedly, he was very weak. He saw something shiny floating, he suspected that it was water. He went for it and tried to get to it. He was surprised, it was spring fresh water, he laughed. He consumed large amounts of the water, and filled out some bottles for Julianne and Kevin. He laughed roughly.

No one there was able to find each other in that cave. They still searched for everybody, unstoppably. It was midnight, only Kevin had a lot of rest, more than the other two. He gasped as he woke up. He was surprised, Timothy was right by him, splashing some water over his face. He was very dehydrated, Timothy gave him a bottle of water. His breathing sound rusty.

"Where is Julianne? Is she ok?" he asked.

"She is somewhere in the cave, I lost her after the horrible events that was upon on us," Timothy said. "Have you found anything?" he asked.

"Yes, I found something very fascinating, and interesting. You will see it later on," he said.

Kevin got up off the ground; his chest had a simple pain. He didn't even know why the pain appeared in his chest. Timothy assumed that he was traumatized after all that had happened. "I cannot leave the cave or look for Julianne. She will be all right for now, let's stay with me, I will take you to the chamber," he said.

"What chamber? Why do you think there is a chamber?" Timothy asked. "You will see, then you will understand more ," Kevin said. They walked, Timothy holding his arm on his shoulder so that he could walk a little quicker.

They entered a creepy chamber room. "Holy shit, this chamber is so enormous. It actually scares me out." Timothy said.

"Yeah, I know. But that is what it looks like in my dreams before. I do recognize the look of it now," Kevin said.

"I guess you will recognize all the answers here to figure out the pieces," Timothy said.

Kevin nodded, and said, "I know." Kevin was ready to face the truth. He assumed he would get all the answers, to know the shocking moments.

There were seven torches, in a circle, in the symbol of a star. Kevin asked Timothy to support him in the center of the symbol.

"Why the center? Do you think you will get answers there?" Timothy asked.

"Just take me there and you pull back a little further from where I am and watch the presentation," Kevin said. He beamed at Timothy. "If anything happens to me, please tell Julianne that I cherish her so much, and tell our new baby all the tales about me. Take care, Timothy," he said.

Kevin was at the center of the symbol; Tiger appeared in blue smoke, standing in front of him. Kevin looked at it real hard. He said, "I am ready, let's hit the show." Tiger's eyes became shimmery, glowing into greenish, then its body decomposed. It surged into his chest; the pain was undoubtedly doubling, more painfully each time.

He appeared to Timothy; his body was shaking like a vibrator. His eyes became solid black. "Oh, my God. This really fucking scares me. I hope he is ok after all of these damnations," he said.

"WATCH THE SHOW, PAY ATTENTION AND BE CAUTIOS, TIMOTHY," Kevin screamed. Timothy walked back into the corner of the dungeon for his safety. He grunted and cried lightly. Darkness had begun.

# Chapter 5

## Truth of the Darkness

As Kevin placed his foot in the center of the star, with 5 blue fires lit. Timothy remained in the corner of the dungeon to see the show. Kevin was no longer shaking, or afraid of anything. He was in low pain, it would enhance the torture. His eyes were growing black, he turned his head to where Timothy was standing.

"Oh, shit. What the fuck did they do to him? I am getting him out of that rotten evil symbol," Timothy said. He ran to Kevin, he struggled to pull him off the stone. Kevin captured him, setting his hands on Timothy's neck, and choking him. He threw him flying and bouncing against the wall.

"DO NOT INTERFERE! YOU WILL GET HURT OR KILLED. STAY A DISTANCE FROM ME, OTHERWISE I WILL HAVE TO KILL YOU," he said. Timothy was outraged and in shock that he would say such things to him. He was injured badly.

Julianne finally remembered the way where she walked down in the direction with the other two. "Finally, I recalled the whole trip, now let's see if I fail," she said. "God damn Kevin; you should realize better I am carrying another life. I do not want it to be hurt." She walked down the same corridor, the ones that have blue burning. All of the fires were disappeared, they would not be ignited again. "Shit, I got to use matches also." She was not that nervous when she was re-taking the trip. She appeared to believe she was brave at that moment. She pursued the same path. Hopefully, she was all right alone by herself.

Kevin's arms were starting to shake and he was in severe pain. He screamed in pain, the blue light appeared right in the center of Kevin, it lit and brightened around him. Timothy was able to see him clearly. His arms looked inhuman; his skin turned into black hairs all over his arms. He roared still. It grew on his skinny body all over, very slowly.

"Is he one of the black cats? Or what?" Timothy thought. Kevin broke down and lay on his knees on the ground. His screams became lighter than before. He opened his eyes and he blinked toward the ground, Timothy couldn't see his face yet. As he dramatically picked up his head, his eyes rolled up and looked at him, he growled. His eyes were greenish just like the others. Timothy breathed hard, hysterical, it horrified him deeply. Kevin pushed off the ground, and got up to stand. He observed himself by his arms first, then everywhere around and on his body. "What the fuck? What happened to me? What have they done to me?" he asked.

He had an instant drowsiness, and blacked out completely. He fell down to the ground very hard. Timothy ran to him, shaking him, and trying to get him to open his eyes. Nothing happened. Timothy gave up and let him alone. He felt it was necessary to go out and find Julianne. She might be helpful in some ways. He left the chamber to search for her. Kevin lay down, looking peaceful. Timothy sighed when he looked at him.

During Kevin's blackout, he was taken into a dreamland. Kevin went into his childhood; he was taken back to years ago. Tiger and Kevin had an ability called "tale". They could read each other's thoughts.

"Here's the beginning of the truth, learn carefully. You will understand more only if you listen to it very hard," She said.

"Yeah? Finally, I get to know more of the truth. I really do want to know what has happened to me lately," he said. "All right. Are you ready?" She asked. He nodded as in, 'Yes'.

Tiger took him back to 1975, before the year Kevin was born. Now truth starts coming. They both stood in Kevin's mother's home. A person, the owner of one black kitten, hands it over to mother. Black Kitten was so little and cute, shiny solid black. Kevin smiled; Tiger picked its head up and looked at him. Everything he saw became blurry and disappeared, a new scene appeared.

The scene was placed at the hospital, when his mother was in labor, ready to give birth to Kevin. Kevin was like, "Wow that was me. This baby is me, isn't he?" He laughed lightly, he was happy. A few seconds later, he saw something very strange, as he looked at the baby (himself), he looked at him, giving a freak look, its eyes suddenly become black. Kevin gasped, "What the hell? What the hell with the eyes?" A nurse walked out carrying the baby. Kevin turned around to follow the nurse, Tiger followed him. When the nurse made the left turn in the hallway. Kevin ran slowly, making the left turn. He slipped and fell down on the floor.

"What the fuck?" He looked at the floor, there was blood all over it. The nurse's neck had been clawed and bleeding as it flowed. "Where is the baby Kevin?" he asked.

"Look behind you. Please," Tiger said. He turned around back behind him, he screamed quickly and short. A black cat walked toward him, with only two legs. "Holy shit. What the fuck is this?" he asked.

"The little black cat is you, the baby has transformed into a black cat," Tiger said.

"What the hell are you talking about?" Kevin asked again.

"You are not only human, but a half human and the other half of a cat. That is what you are," Tiger said. As the little black cat got closer to him, it transformed back into a human baby. "Oh, my God. Who am I? Where do I come from? Tiger, tell me. This is getting me really freaked," Kevin said.

All of a sudden, he was taken to the present scene. Timothy and Julianne cannot see him and Tiger. Kevin and Tiger walked down to the chamber. He looked at himself lying on the floor, he is in the form of a black cat, he had all black fur over his body, different clothes, and his eyes were exactly like a cat.

"How did all of this start? I want to know more about my genetics." he asked.

"You will be told more and learn more later," It said.

The dreamland had ended. Kevin woke up, got up off the ground. He saw Timothy lying down at the corner of the chamber. He stood still and smiled at Timothy. He turned his head from right to left, as right he is human, when he made a move to the left slowly, he became a black cat, the clothes suddenly changed. He laughed aloud, inside his body, he was very angry. He walked toward Timothy, he was shaking when Kevin came closer to him. Surprised, he offered his hand to Timothy, to take his hand. Kevin pulled him out of the corner, helping him to stand properly. He was in the form of a black cat, he smiled toward him. Timothy began to calm the shakes he was having.

He carried Timothy with him into the next room after the chamber room. Julianne happened to be in a dungeon, just a few blocks away from the chamber room. She continued to search for them both. She no longer sobbed, trying to be brave, knowing what to expect at the next step. All of the sudden, everywhere, in the whole of the cave, torches were lit with blue fires. She felt better, now she could see clearly, but in a bluish view. She laughed. She took an instant rest.

"Where are you taking me? Where are we now?" Tim asked.

"I am taking you to where the truth lies. I want you to see what I have been through and to understand what the whole story is all about," Kevin said.

"Oh, I would love that, it would be great," Timothy laughed.

"Ah, we are here now. I am putting you down on the ground, take a break, I will go check out something, be right back," he said. Timothy nodded as in 'yes'.

Kevin looked at Timothy, without him realizing. His eyes were so devilish, greenish, looking very angry. He went a little farther into a very dark area. Timothy would be able to see his eyes glow greenly. He preferred not to interfere with what he was doing. He kept his mind to himself. Kevin did not return for an hour. When Kevin found a dark area, he sat down and thought a lot of what was going on.

"Was this just a truth, or is there more to it? What was I supposed to do next?" he said to himself. Tiger faded in, looking at him. She intended that Kevin follow its step to find the more revealing truth.

He saw several very old albums, which contained many pictures and letters. He looked through the very first album, found some pictures of his father, he was puzzled by some writing on the back of the picture, it said "Tiger".

"Is Tiger my father? What's going on?" he said to himself. Tiger was stand next to him, meowing to get his attention, as he turned his head to Tiger, Tiger transformed into a human, he looked a little old.

"Hey, son. It has been a long time. Yes, I am your father," Tiger said. "

"What are you talking about? Are you really my father, if so, how come I have never seen you since I was a baby," he said. "I feel more comfortable being a cat instead of a human. You should know the rest of story, by what happened to me? Don't you remember anything at all?"

"Yes, I remember that my mother killed you by drowning you in the swimming pool. Is that correct?"

"You got that right. I don't know why she would do such thing like that to me."

They both hugged and had a long conservation. "Let's get out of here. It has been a very long day for all of us, and I have to find Julianne. You are going to be a grandfather soon," Kevin said. "Oh. Let's find them first then we all can get out of here," Tiger said. They smiled at each other.

As Julianne sat down on the ground, looking very nasty and dirty. She was not even moving at all, there were a couple of black cats standing watching her, staring, their eyes were glowing red. She knew they were so devilish. She refused to make any moves or sounds until she was found.

Kevin, Tiger and Timothy walked out into the chamber, finally, they found Julianne sitting down on the ground, all dirty all over her body, smelly with a strong odor. Julianne screamed loudly, roughly, when she saw a large black cat walking toward her. Timothy ran to her and calmed her down, he explained everything to her, "He is Kevin, your boyfriend. He was transformed into a black cat, because there is a reason to it. Do you understand?" Timothy said.

She panted, shivering feeling scared. She nodded as in Okay. "Let's get out of here now before dark. Everyone ready?" said Tiger.

"Why do we need to be ready to get out of here?" Julianne asked. "Tiger is my father, it's a long story, I will tell you later," Kevin said.

"Because there may be violence coming among us as we walk out of here, I just don't know what it is," Tiger said.

Fade in, fade out, all black cats with red glowing eyes, and walking up to them. "Freeze. Be quiet now. I smell something out front of us," Tiger growled. He and Kevin, suddenly jumped into an unseen spot, clawing something that no one could see. Black cats with red eyes faded in, and began the battle. Julianne and Timothy ran for their lives, working on their way out of the woods. Tiger and Kevin still remained there to end the battle. The battle became very gruesome, and too gory. The gore, no one would able to stand, and watch. Julianne groaned, and fell down on the ground, "My belly cramps, it hurts like hell."     "Let's up and keep on running, we will worry about that later," Timothy said.

Timothy and Julianne had enough energy to keep running without any stopping, to leave the woods. Tiger and Kevin, they both became very delighted in the violence in the battle. They had successfully killed most of them, some were still around. They did not have the ability to see the souls yet. Especially Kevin, he was bleeding, losing a large amount of blood. His temper had gone completely uncontrollable. He screamed angrily, Tiger went to stop him somehow. He stopped him because he thought it was necessary to prevent his anger into becoming a devastated one.

"Hey, Tiger, listen to me. Go get these two out of the woods; I will take care of this. Just go," said Kevin.

"Are you sure? Can you handle the numbers of these?"

"Yes, I can. Get the fuck out of here now. GO!" said Kevin. Tiger ran pretty fast, jumping and bouncing against the trees repeatedly. Tiger looked at him far away, he turned his head to the crowd of red-eyed black cats, and he smiled, "It's time." He draws his swords from both sides. He laughed screeching loudly. Tiger suddenly stopped and looked back, "Good luck", then he left.

Kevin felt that the sword would really help the battle to end. He attacked many of them with swords. He closed his eyes, still bleeding. He was thinking of many things that were positive, something that was so precious to him, he just screamed in pain in his whole body. He now acquired a special ability, he could see the souls everywhere. He somehow could tell that his body was being shaken in small steps, it grew and grew. His body became a little roughly shaken, he drew his swords up in the air, and screamed the loudest, everywhere around him, everyone around him could hear a frightening sound. Something blue and white flashed, exploding out of his body, it attacked and killed completely the set of black ones with red glowing eyes.

He just faded out without a trace. Tiger saddened, found Timothy and Julianne. "Kevin's gone to save us. He told me to look after you to be sure you guys are out of danger. I am sorry." Tiger sobbed lightly.

"No. No. No," she sobbed as hard as rock.

"I am sorry," Timothy said.

"Let's go, we will call it for the day, wait and see," Tiger said. He hugged Julianne tightly. "Why has all of this to happen? What caused all those nightmares he is having?" she asked. "Because it's fate, and it is truth," Tiger said.

They were lurking out of the woods, unharmed. They all looked very disappointed and saddened. They also had a good cry. They headed to Kevin's place, and rested there until further. His place looked too gory from the event a few days ago. They intended to clean up everything. They hoped to hear something about Kevin. Their concerns had been increased a high amount.

Kevin lay down on the ground, out of energy; nothing could get him to open his eyes or mouth. It had been 3 days after the battle was ended. He looked truly dead, when he fiercely opened his right eye quickly. He gasped for air, breathing hard to get some air. His body was trying to heal all the wounds itself. He must not move at all until it was healed completely, first.

# Chapter 6

## Resurrected

Kevin's wound had been healing completely after 8 days from the terminated battle. It was quite certainly a long time for him. He breathed deeply, making sighing sounds . He opened his eyes; it hurt his eyes, because the day was too bright. He groaned as he looked at his lower body, "Thank God, I am back in human form," he laughs. He got up and stood clumsily; his legs weren't exactly ready to be held.

As he walked away smiling, he faded away as if he was a ghost. He arrived at his place, barged into the place. There was Julianne asleep on the sofa, shivering. He looked at her face; rubbing her face lightly with one of his thumbs. Her face made a tiny movement. He took one of his coverings, and put the cover on her, to keep her warm. He then took a good shower, doing a major clean up in the apartment. Julianne remained resting. Timothy was at his home, sitting outside on the lanai; waiting to receive word from Kevin. He cried slowly, lightly.

Julianne sniffed; she smelled something like Clorox bleaches. It woke her, she looked puzzled at the look of the neat living room.

She was alarmed, believing someone was inside the apartment. She walked slowly into the hall, seeing a shadow move. She picked up the bulky kitchen knife, and put it into her fist. She walked to the area where she saw the shadow. Kevin scared her by directly confronting her, he smiled. "You scared the shit out of me, what were you thinking of doing with that?" She smacked his chest, yelling.

"I assumed you were dead. Where were you?" Julianne asked.

"I let my injuries restore fully, and my energy be regenerated. So I will be fiercer than before," he said.

Julianne, her eyes were tearful and shiny while she looked at his eyes. "No matter what, I will always love you, even if you are a cat," she said. They both hugged each other tightly, and beamed at each other.

"As for your information, I am undead. I do not have a heartbeat at all. Do you follow?" he said.

"What are you trying to say?"

"I died back in battle, somehow I am back alive for some reason," he said.

"Can I feel your heartbeat?" she asked.

"Go ahead, remember, my heart is yours," Kevin said. She smiled kindly.

Timothy appeared at the front door. He didn't know about Kevin, until he answered the door. He screamed eerily.

"What the hell happened to you? I supposed you were dead, weren't you?" he said.

Kevin laughed. "It is a long story. But at least I am all right," he said to Timothy.

"You scared the hell out of me, you know that I can't live with you," Timothy said.

"Got it." he said.

"Whew. Julianne, are you all right?" he asked.

"Yes, I am all right, just woke up because Kevin was cleaning up the place. It startled me; I thought he was someone else." She laughed.

"Hey, heed, all of you. Just as you should know, the battle recently ended. But the end is just the beginning. It has not been over yet. There will be many battles coming up soon."

"WHAT? What do you mean? How come it is not over? I thought you finished them off, didn't you?" Timothy and Julianne said.

"I thought the war was over, but I could sense a strong presence and my gut feelings that it is not over yet," Kevin said.

Tiger returned, "It's time to go, and they are coming. We got to go somewhere and be prepared for anything," he said.

"How do I know if I am going to change into a black cat?" Kevin asked.

"You will see. Use your mind, body, and your spirit only when required. You will have to figure it out yourself," Tiger said.

"I got it. I got to learn them myself, is that what you are saying?" he said.

"You got that right," Tiger said. "All of you three, like I instructed before, be ready for anything," he said.

The windows in the lounge and the deck windows were instantly blown up, they all inspected the panes that were blown up; there were some black cats with red eyes. Kevin told everyone not to move, to freeze, do not fear.

"The black cats with red eyes are called "Magus' Servant". They are lethal; they eliminate anything that got in their way, or even if it didn't. They can smell our fear, if they do, they will attack us fast without us knowing."

There was 13 of Magus' Servants walking around the place, one of them sitting down to look at Tiger casually, like a hawk would do. As if it has the capacity to see him clearly. Tiger recognized it glaring at him, he closed his eyes slowly. And he looked away from it.

"What's going on with them?" Julianne asked.

"Don't talk, don't move and I will explain later. Just do whatever to remain quiet otherwise you will get murdered," Kevin said.

The Servants went to the group, and smelled them carefully, sniffing several times. Somehow, Kevin began shaking terribly. Few of the Servants were restrained, and looked around at him, walking steadily, growling.

"He was converted into a black cat." They screamed in growls, he drew his blade, he grinned.

"Give me your best shot. I am going to smash your heads dearly," he said.

"You better finish them all, damn it," Julianne said.

"Get out of here while you can. GO NOW," Kevin said.

"I am staying with you until end of the battle," Tiger said.

"All right, suit yourself," he said.

"Such attitude, same old shit," Tiger said and laughed. They both began the battle. Tiger had a metal claw on both of his hands. "Are you ready? I am," he said.

"Of course, I am always ready. Why?" Kevin asked. He drew his shiny sword. During the jumps, the Servants were trying, Kevin's sword cut three of them in a row, an instant attack. He cut them in half. These three fell down in pieces on the floor and burned, decomposed.

"Oh, I see. It looks like you have bettered your skill with the blade, haven't you?" Tiger said.

"Doesn't that surprise you? I learned fast, didn't I? Kevin replied. The six Servants ran toward Tiger immediately.

"Let me take care of them. Watch my show," he said and smiled, nodding. He successfully clawed all of the six Servants. They also decomposed and faded away. "Damn, I am too old for this shit; it has gotten easier for me than before. I am getting bored with it," he said.

"What made you think this is funny?" Kevin asked.

"Because I have been to this battle a thousand times before and it seems never ending," Tiger said.

"Oh, I see," Kevin scoffed.

"Let's finish them, whatever's left, together." Both agreed. The Servants jumped toward them, attacking them gruesomely. But one of them bit Kevin's arm. It made him angry and he stabbed its head with his sword. "Damn, where did they come from? Do you know?" Kevin asked.

"That is what I have been asking myself since I first saw them," Tiger said. "We will find out soon, won't we?"

"Yes, we will. We ought to recover more information as rapidly as we can, before it is too late," Kevin said.

Julianne and Timothy were waiting in the hall. "Hey, didn't I already tell you to leave here? Why didn't you guys listen to me?" Kevin said.

"God, they would have gotten themselves killed," Tiger said. "I am sorry. I thought we would be safe in the hall, close to you." Both said.

"All right, at least you guys are still alive. But next time, do what I say, whether you like it or not. Got my drift?" Kevin said. They kept their lips sealed.

"I assume we will have to retreat to the Cave of Cat's Eye, to learn the whereabouts of these Magus' Servants. We need to find it before it expands everywhere," Tiger said.

"Shit. Let's get everything we need for the repeated trip." Timothy said.

"Why is this happening again? I didn't even get a solution as to why," Julianne said and sobbed slightly. Kevin held her strongly, and said, "Calm down. Take it easy. Everything will be fine. You need to be strong, please remember you are carrying a child. Like I said, I will never let anything happen to you and our child. Remember that," he said.

They left the place, on the way back to the Cave of Cat's Eye. They took a car, to save their time and all of the troubles. They damaged the vehicle while on the trip. Timothy drove the car through the woods, causing large amounts of debris. "I don't give a fuck about the car. I just want this to be over," he said.

"I agree, but it is not as easy as it looks. There is bloodshed and death involved, it is something you could not stand," Tiger said. "You do not know how to kill them, do you? If you do not understand any of this, do not attempt to fight or anything, it could be more harmful to both of you," he said.

"Do not get in our way, or their way at this time, if we need help, we will let you know.," Kevin said.

"I got your drift. I will keep Julianne safe somewhere until further. That is something I can do for you right now," Timothy said.

"Thank you. I appreciated that," Kevin said. "Please stay with Timothy, one way or another. Can you promise me that?" he asked.

"Okay, I promise. I swear," she said.

"Why can't he let me do something about it? At least I can help at something," she was thinking. She saddened, and looked worry, biting her nails nervously.

"Hey. Cheer up. There will be something we can help with. We will figure it out as soon as we arrive there. Do not worry about that right now." Timothy smiled.

"Don't smile at me like everything is going all right," she said angrily.

"Whoa. Nothing new about women. They are not easy to deal with, are they?" Timothy was thinking.

They approached the Cave of Cat's Eye. They suddenly stopped and moved out of the vehicle. There were numerous Magus

Servants guarding the cave entrance. Kevin was angry, he drew his silver sword. He ran toward the Servants, his speed was like nitro. He faded away then reappeared repeatedly, in many different positions. Tiger drew his claws, making several show off moves. "Let's bleed them." Kevin said.

Julianne shuddered and locked all doors and closed the windows. She actually hated anything with red eyes. "Calm down, and do not move at all, so they won't see us, or dice us any way they like," Timothy said.

Suddenly her face turned a little blue, she was sweating, gasping lightly for air. Timothy was sweating. All the windows were closed, so inside the car turned into some heat. Timothy looked drowsy, and was about to check to see Julianne to be sure she was all right.

"JULIANNE, BREATH, BREATH," he shouted. He took a great risk and opened a window, so Julianne could be able to breath. She looked very blue, continuing to gasp for air. He checked the back of the car to see if anything would help, he found a bottle of water. The bottled water wasn't exactly cold, but a little between cool and warm. He poured the water into her mouth, her mouth was pretty much blue and white. He panted, saying, "Don't you dare die on me. I need you to breath. Hey, Julianne wake up." Her bluish face went down slowly. "Oh, God. She's all right, so is her pregnancy. Whew," he said.

She finally gasped for air, and her breath became stable. She was still breathing a bit heavy. At least, she was all right just for now. She was sleeping, she had lost all of her energy, and was truly very tired.

Kevin was bleeding them, he had killed more than a few dozen. Tiger successfully killed several; somehow he got a bad deep scratch in the lower belly. He began to tire, and lost his balance, his energy had gone unbalanced. "Hey Dad, are you all right? You look injured, are you?" Kevin asked.

"Hell no, I am not all right. Yeah, I am injured, help me. I am about to black out," he said. Kevin dropped his sword, and ran to his dad before Tiger fell down to the ground. He grabbed him, lying him down gently. "I will go get help now, I will be right back. Hold on," he said. Timothy was sitting on the hood outside, smoking a cigarette . Julianne was sleeping.

Timothy saw Kevin running toward him. He knew that he needed help right away. So, he got in the vehicle quickly and drove it.

He crashed into the cave. Julianne bumped her head onto the dashboard painfully. They all three searched for Tiger, and carried him out of the cave. Julianne tried to keep pressure on where he had bad scratches or cuts.

"You two keep him alive until I come back. I am going in to finish what has started. Got it?" Kevin said. Timothy nodded. Julianne cried lightly.

Kevin went back inside the cave; He slashed as many as he could. Especially one of the Servants stronger ones; he had such difficulty defeating it. The Servant went invisible repeatedly, that caused Kevin to miss while he was trying to attack it. He suddenly fell unconscious, and then his body shook as if it was having a seizure. He acquired a new ability, which was invisibility. He wondered how he received it, he would find his answer later, he thought he needed to finish the battle the best he could. He eventually lost his temper, he now showed his anger which the Servant did not understand. It gave him more advantage to destroy it.

He got on his leg by "bending" standing, he started growling. He rolled his eyes up a little, his pupils became shrank, and his eyes were suddenly solid black. He had completely forgotten all of his pains; his strength had been uprising more powerful. He ran very fast using his invisibility repeatedly, to confuse the Servant. Sp came the scene, the Servant couldn't see him, he appears behind its back, and growling lightly, the Servant turned around, screeching loudly, and he slashed it, sword shining. He turned around and walked away with his body floating. He continued walking away and faded away.

Timothy screamed loudly, annoying everyone. Kevin ran out of the cave before it collapsed on itself. Tiger breathed slowly, gasping for breath. He asked for Kevin. He walked toward his father. He bent his legs and lay, kneeling on the ground.

"Listen, son, it still is not over. You need to find more truth and you need to talk to your mother to find out more details, do you understand?" Tiger said.

"Yes, I do understand what you are trying to imply," Kevin said. "Hey, Timothy, can you get the car to start?" he asked.

"I will see if I can," Timothy said.

Tiger sighed heavily. "You will be all right. Take it easy. Julianne will help fix your wounds," said Kevin.

"I will take care of you, I promise. You will be fine." Julianne was smiling. The cave collapsed, but there was something fishy, Kevin looked at the cave. He could still feel its presence. He assumed something was still alive inside the cave. As Kevin turned around, he noticed something about Tiger. His scratches were attempting to heal slowly. All of sudden, Tiger has a shock himself, his breathing stopped, his eyes were open wide, not in motion. He was frozen completely, looking very dead. Kevin was extremely upset, he got closer to Tiger. "You are a son of bitch. You fucked us up. See you later," Kevin said.

He picked him up and put him on his shoulder, carried him to where Kevin was dead earlier. He put him down gently and said, "Goodbye". He smiled, walking away from him, "Leave him there, we will take care of him later on. Let's get out of here," he said.

"Yeah, we need a big break for the day," Timothy said. Julianne groaned and cried in pain. She rubbed her belly. The baby moved around and stretched itself, making her very uncomfortable. "You go to the car, rest there for a while; we will come get you, okay?" Timothy said.

Julianne got in the car, in the front, waiting for them, she rested her eyes until later. She was about to doze off. Kevin and Timothy went back to where they put Tiger's body. "Aw, shit. He disappeared, let's get out of here," Timothy said.

"Calm down, I may know where he is going right now. I think his wound has been healed," Kevin said. "Let's get out of here, and get back to Julianne before anything comes up," he said. They left the area, and headed back to the car. They were puzzled, Julianne was not in the car, and she was gone. "I hope Tiger has not gotten her, let's find her," Timothy said.

"I think he has captured her, let's gather everything we need, then we start searching for her. I might as well as have to battle with my father when I find him," Kevin said.

"Oh, no. Not again," Timothy said.

# Chapter 7

## Tiger's Second Death

A few hours later, they had already gathered everything; they were out of their strength, but not giving up. So, they began their search for Julianne, and Tiger. They understood that their car was totaled, unfixable. They had no choice but endless searching on their own feet. Kevin sniffed, he could smell something, he awaited. Tiger jumped out of nowhere, landing on the ground by his knees, his head was downward, as he picked up his head, his eyes so rosy. He growled, glaring at them, and he attempted to start a combat with Kevin.

He instantly stopped, and stood still. He was getting ready to draw his blade, but he would rather wait for Tiger to respond first. He had his hand by the blade, waiting to capture it. Both of them stood still, not making any movements. There was growling. "Why are you not making any steps? Oh I get it. Was I supposed to make the first move? Is it not what you were trying to tell me?" Tiger said.

"Figure it out yourself; I am not talking too much like you. You are just some big mouth; I am going to skewer you one way or another," Kevin said. Tiger looked very gruesome, drooling. He made a very first left, running like a mouse, and jumping toward Kevin when he was not in front of him. Tiger was screeching, cutting his blade at him when Tiger surged closer to him.

Tiger blew in roars after he was winded. He fell on the ground, looking up at his son Kevin. "You may have slayed me, I will always be back for you. Are you gutsy enough to kill me and to be sure that I am fallen?" Tiger said.

"Hmm. I am not sure, you are not fighting yourself, you are my father, Tiger, and you allow it to control you. But if you insist, I will be more than glad to kill you without any remorse or regards. Do you understand?" Kevin said.

Tiger laughed. "Go ahead and kill me if you must," he said.

"My pleasure. Let's finish this," Kevin said. Tiger got himself up and stood. He drew his claws, and moved his thumb, in a "Come on" gesture. Kevin grinned, and walked with caution, with his blade to defend himself. He became invisible, Tiger growled as in surprise. He became very defensive. Kevin appeared behind him, and cut him by the blade, he was unstoppable. Tiger roared in pain. "Finally, you got me. You have gotten stronger and stronger." Tiger laughed. He fell down to the ground worn out, and bleeding strongly. His son walked to him, sitting by the knee.

"It is all right, it's painless, close your eyes." Tiger insisted to remain alert; he wanted to tell him something.

"I should have told you everything a long time ago and I should have never left you with your mother. I felt real terrible."

"None of this would have happened if you told me before, I would have gotten a handle of what I am going through."

"I am sorry to put you through so much pain.

"I'm better off dead, and you need to complete what you started. Even you are going to have a baby who is a boy."

"Yes, I am going to finish whatever it takes, and how do you know if it is boy?"

"Trust me on this; you are going to be great father and teacher to your son." Tiger closed his eyes, and his breathing stopped. Kevin picked him up and held him tightly.

"I will be seeing you soon, meanwhile, do not go away just yet," he said.

He carried his father in his arms, walking to a place where Julianne and Timothy were expecting them. As soon as Julianne saw him carrying his father, she ran, full of fear and grievances, several of her tears fell or poured on Tiger, and the tears were shining, shimmering.

"I love you, I promise you I will take care of Kevin, and our child," she sobs. She held him very tightly. "I will see you soon," she said. Timothy sniffed, attempting to cry but he held back, trying not to cry or to be distressed.

"Why did you have to kill him? What made you do this?" he asked. "I had no choice but to kill him, sadly. He urged to be killed, I gave him his wish. I am not sorry for what I did," Kevin said.

Timothy scoffed. "Damn you, you should know better than that. Don't touch me, please," she insisted. Kevin kept his hands to himself. He let her alone for a while. They all walked out of the woods, and took Tiger to his place for now. Kevin returned to human form, he sighed. "Whoa, I am so lightheaded. I need to sit down, rest a few minutes," he said. "Hey, take it easy. We will wait for you to feel a little better, and then we need to go to your place, and figure out where to give him a proper burial, don't we?" Timothy said.

They arrived at Kevin's place, they bundled Tiger with the blankets, and put him on the couch. They took a short break, discussing the proper burial. Kevin was thinking of having him cremated, to release the soul and let him rest in peace. Julianne and Timothy agreed. They waited until night, so no one was able to see in the night. Dark had come, they were eager to be ready, taking his body to the ocean where no one would inspect or visit. Kevin put him on the wood nicely. He set a fire underneath his body, and lit it. He didn't put any fuel or any kind of liquid on him. He felt it is a disgrace, and a blasphemy. Let the body burn itself, they stayed there all night until the body was absolutely ash.

At the dawn, Julianne was sleeping on the sand, she woke up. Timothy and Kevin were already awake as usual. They discussed many things, "I am excited to be a father soon, I could not wait to play and raise my son," Kevin said.

"Who says anything about the child being a boy? What makes you think it is a boy?" she asks.

"My father said to trust him that it is boy," he smiled.

Julianne smiled and snickered. She held him tightly, "Like I said, I love you no matter what."

"I love you, too. I will ensure nothing will happen to you," he said.

They said something as a farewell to Tiger. They left the funeral, and returned to their home. They had not spoken to each other for a day or two. That evening, at nighttime, Julianne was at home, cooking her own dinner. Something went poof, she felt cold inside the kitchen, she felt something bother her, and she decided to look out the windows, as she carefully looked through the windows, she suddenly screamed, there was a Servant, snarling, jumping right to the window. The windows were cracked, and breaking. The Servant suddenly disappeared. Julianne fell down into the corner; she took a knife, holding it. She looked around the kitchen, then walked to the living room, nothing was there. She panted, sighing, "Thank God." She swept the kitchen where the windows were surrendering. She felt an urge to see her fiancée.

She went to Kevin's place, thumping on the door, it was not answered. It concerned her, "Maybe he went to see Timothy, I'll go there," She thought. She went to his place. Timothy was sitting on the porch, drinking his favorite lemonade juice. They both have no idea of the whereabouts of Kevin. They started to worry.

"Maybe he returned to the graveyard or the collapsed cave?"

"Should we go over there?" she asked. They would want to investigate to be sure. They took a drive there.

There was Kevin. He was sitting and looking at the broken cave quietly.

"Are you okay? What are you doing here?" she asked.

"It is not over; I have had quite a few interrupted nightmares last night. It seems I cannot get rid of them," he said.

"Oh I see, I had an incident with a Servant this morning in my kitchen. It broke my window. It scared the hell out of me."

"Hey you both have a lot to deal with right now. I have not had any incidents or nightmares since your dad died," Timothy said.

"Because you are not part of my family. We are, also carrying a child who has our blood, it will never go away, I assume" Kevin said. They knew that it would never be over, they don't know how to conclude it. They pursued to go before studying it. "We should do what my dad told us to. We need to put an end to it. I would like to do that to honor his requests. Will you two?" Kevin said.

"Yes, let's do it," Timothy and Julianne said at the same time.

Kevin dug up the cave, to find a hole to retrieve the cave. Julianne and Timothy located a shovel in the car. They were aiding him dig the cave. Kevin believed there was something he was missing, or overlooked inside the cave before. He expected to retrieve it; he was not sure of what it was. "I will find what I am looking for, but let's find the access first." Kevin said. He smiled at his fiancée.

It took them hours to find an entrance. They succeeded in finding the entrance to the cave. They went into the entrance. Again, the pathway was lit by a blue flame. It sounded like they were expecting Kevin to come back. "It's remaining the same, but I can see some modifications around here. Let's go explore other areas of the cave, see if we find anything useful," Timothy said. They split up and explored everywhere. Kevin went back to where the chamber was, when he was inside the chamber, he transformed into a black cat again. He found a door in the chamber room; he opened it, and entered. The room was very dark, luckily, a blue flame was lit; there was a blue saber lying on the ground with light toward it. He went for it, and stood by the new saber. He picked it up and the saber was alight itself, a very bright blue light. He discarded the old sword, and put the saber on his back. He felt enhanced, more powerful and with some new abilities.

He left the room, and walked back to the entrance of the chamber room. Something whispered loudly, he turned around and saw the center symbol glowing. He walked to the center of it. And he drew the saber, it was glowing. He knew something was coming up. He closed his eyes and was quiet. The glowing mini orbs were flying around him, and his body gravitated all of the orbs into its body. He became very much fiercer; he also acquired some souls of black cats.

Julianne and Timothy did not find anything worthy to study at the moment. They left the cave, and waited outside.

"I do not know why we weren't able to find anything. Where is Kevin?"

"I think he's still exploring around to find something. It's really important to him, isn't it?" she said. Kevin climbed out of the entrance. He was in human form. The saber was invisible when he was human, it would appearing once he became a black cat.

The saber was actually Tiger's. Kevin was given the saber to keep Tiger's soul alive, and to remember him. It was enhanced with spirits inside it. It was unbreakable. The Servants are looking for the saber because they thought it would give them more power than ever before. Kevin did not know that they were looking to acquire it.

"Hey, did you find something there?" Timothy asked.

"Yeah I found it; it was the blue saber Tiger left me," Kevin said. "Let's get out of here for now. We will return here later," he said.

"What are we going to do now?" Timothy asked.

"Nothing until later. Meanwhile, we rest and do whatever we want," Kevin said.

"Let's go home, I need to rest, I am tired," Julianne said.

"All right, let's get going. You, Timothy, go home and enjoy your evening. Got it?" Kevin said.

Timothy nodded, and proceeded straight home. They both walked to Kevin's place. They had a good pleasant evening. There were no horrible incidents, or tortures that nighttime.

# Chapter 8

## Endless of Nightmares

Since Tiger's death, no one had any recurring dreams or tortures. Kevin felt a lot more relaxed. Julianne did some orchards outside her home. Timothy remained the same, sitting on the lanai in front of his home. They all beamed. Kevin lay down and rested as usual. That nighttime, Timothy was sleeping with all the windows open. He kipped very hard, but was very sensitive with his nose. He sniffed, there was a rotten odor getting closer to him.

He woke up, observed a Servant sitting on the couch, watching him. He was struggling, and shouted at it. He was very scare, shocked, the cat walked slowly to his leg, and kept walking toward him. He choked and felt concussed like he was having a seizure. The cat landed on him between his neck and chest. It opened its mouth and cried, attacking him by biting. Timothy suddenly defended himself with his arms covering. It eventually disappeared.

Julianne woke up, she was thirsty for water. She walked to the kitchen, perplexed, glass was all over the kitchen floor. The windows were shattered and broken. She knew she did clean them up before. She thought it might be just a dream, she neglected it, and went to the fridge, as she opened the door, "Ahh" she screamed. There were dozens of black cats' head with red eyes lying down on the entire shelf. They all moved their mouths and jawbones. She slammed the door, reversing a little. She shivered, she risked opening the door again. It was also disappeared as if nothing had taken place. There were foods, drinks, nothing gory.

Kevin dozed off accidentally. A few hours later, late at night, he woke up smelling something very rotten and full of bloodshed. He looked outside through the front windows. He saw more than a few dozen Servants standing looking at the windows. He roared, losing his tempers, and running out of the building, and all the Servants disappeared. Eventually, not strangely for these three people, they went and found each other, and rejoined. They had a long conservation. They thought everything was back to normal.

"Remember I told you, nothing is over yet, and a friend of mine told me once if you have nightmares, it will never go away whether you like it or not. No one is able to find a solution to prevent the nightmares," Kevin said.

"Really? I was told that nightmares can be remedied or treated? I am confused," Timothy said.

"Yeah I agree with Timothy as well," said Julianne. "Well there are all different nightmares, but for this one, nothing can be done," said Kevin.

Kevin could basically deal with it while the others could not. They all stayed over at Kevin's place, because most of the time, Servants, among other things consistently came up at his place. They persisted there for a week. One of these night, Timothy opened the freezer, there was a black cat frozen inside, he shrieked. Kevin rushed to him, "What happened?"

"Look in the freezer, there's a frozen black cat inside," Timothy said. Kevin opened the freezer door, the black cat sat there, growling and hedging in on him, but before it touched Kevin, it disappeared.

Julianne was still sleeping. Nothing occurred to her that night. But next day after the episode, she had a good shower, she usually closed her eyes while she took a shower. The tub was snapping, and cranking, she looked down the tub with water covering her. She rubbed it off so she could see what was down there. The black cat tried to crawl out of the tub pipe, it scared her, and she escaped the shower in a panicked way. She hollered for Kevin, he came in the bathroom where it was happening. He looked at the tub, there was nothing going on there.

"There is nothing down there. What did you see?"

"I saw the black cat crawl out of tub drainer. I broke out of the tub as quickly as I could," she said.

The last night of the stay over, there was a presence, Kevin could sense it. Everyone was sleeping, except Kevin. He still got nightmares or could see things while he was alert. He walked outside on the roof of the building. He walked around to search the grounds by the view from the roof. He did not see anything there, but was still able to feel it. He moved around and attempted to get to the door, while he was doing that. Too many Servants ran from other places to his building, he couldn't hear because they were too quite. He got back inside and went to bed. Meanwhile, the Servants were still lurking around.

Julianne and Timothy were already up. "You better look outside the window. There are plenty of black cats outside lying around, whatever they were doing," said Julianne.

"What? That cannot be. Because I just got back from the roof, I investigated; there are no black cats anywhere," Kevin said.

"Well, look at it now. They may have appeared after you got back inside," Timothy said.

As he looked outside the windows.

"Oh that smells. What are they doing there? Are they going to eat us alive? Or what?" Kevin said.

"Well, let's stay inside for the night, and see what happens in the morning," said Julianne. They insisted on staying inside until they were gone. Timothy walked to the door and opened it. He looked down at the floor, there were two Servants decomposing, hissing. He quickly closed the door. He fell back against the wall, panting.

"What's going on?" Julianne asked.

"There are black cats at the door; I closed it as quick as I could. They look dead, dissolved or something like that," Timothy said. Kevin went to the door and opened it. There were a dozen black cats sit on the floor, waiting for him. He shouted at them, kicking, grabbing them and threw them cruelly. He closed the door promptly.

"Do not open doors or any windows at all. It is too risky opening them right now, let's calm down," Timothy said.

In the morning, Julianne already woke up, she was cooking a breakfast for everyone. The smell of breakfast woke up them both. They stretched themselves, and went to the kitchen.

"Hey, how long have you been up?" Kevin asked.

"Just a few hours, I couldn't get any sleep. I have been so fussy all night," she said. "You all need to get to eat; it will do you good for the day," she said. "Here are your omelets, and biscuits. I will kick your butt if you waste any of it." She smiled.

There were no black cats outside. They were delighted about that. Timothy blacked out and fell down on the floor, and bumped his head hard. He woke up inside the dream. He walked in a very dark place, like a space. There was absolutely nothing around. He looked around and kept walking nowhere, then he began to see several red eyes of the black cats. It was growing and growing, till it becomes countless of them. Timothy lit his lighter, he held the lighter and walked toward them, trying to find a way out. He saw something very shiny and glowing red, he walked toward it, and he moved the lighter to it, it screeched and surged on him. It scratched his face, it was gruesome.

"Oh my God, he is inside his dreams, he got scratches on his face as if a ghost did this without us actually seeing it," Julianne said.

While inside his dream, he screamed and hollered for help. There was no one to help him; he kept running, trying not to look back. Many black cats were still chasing him, screeching and hissing. He had been assaulted many times, hurting his face, chest, back, even his legs. Nothing could stop the black ones from attacking him. His body kept scarring and bleeding as Julianne and Kevin watched. Kevin had no idea on how to stop it. He was trying to shake him, and slap him several times. Timothy had no response to the assault Kevin made on him. Kevin took a risk, and took out his saber, and stabbed it through Timothy's nearby rib. He disappeared from the dream, and returned to normal. He woke up from the blackout.

Kevin took him to hospital, had him stitched on the cut Kevin made on him. He was lucky to be alive, but injured. If Kevin had not done that, he would have probably died.

"Thank you for saving my life, unfortunately, you owe me a big one for stabbing me," Timothy said.

"Yeah, I know. I am sorry but I had no choice, but to do it," Kevin chuckled. Timothy was to remain in hospital for a few days. Julianne gave him a gentle cheek kiss, and said, "See you later, take care."

"It seems that all of us had nightmares, none of us can get rid of, it or restrain it," Kevin said. "I predict it is accurate that no one can stop the nightmares or dreams," she said.

"I reckon I would call that, "Endless Nightmares", is it not?" he said.

# Chapter 9

## Newborn Son

A summer night later, Julianne's pregnancy was showing big. She was setting up a warm Jacuzzi. She poured her favorite bath beads; Rosemary. She undressed herself, but had difficulty in pulling her legs up to go in the Jacuzzi. She was breathing roughly, but finally succeeded in boarding the Jacuzzi. Julianne lay down, smiled, and felt so comfortable. "Time has gone so fast like a housefly; a baby is coming in a few weeks," she thought. She was nauseous and fell asleep in the Jacuzzi.

She was chilled, waking slowly, groaning. She looked down at the water with a large amount of white bubbles, she cleared the bubbles right in front of her with her hands. Her pupils expanded large, and she shuddered. There was a black cat under the water, staring at her, swimming very slowly toward her. The black cat jumped out of the water screaming. Julianne grabbed the cat; trying to toss it out of the Jacuzzi. The black cat screeched, dissolved itself and decomposed. Julianne screamed and noticed there was a lot of blood over the water.

She suddenly jumped out of the Jacuzzi, crying, and heading down to where her belly was bleeding unstoppably. Then came the sobs, "Where the hell is Kevin?" she said. She held her belly and walked a bit at a time. She succeeded in making it to the door, she unlocked the doorknob, there was a black cat -Kevin- right in her face. She fell down, Kevin grabbed her, and the bleeding wouldn't stop. Eventually, the water was broken, he picked her up and carried her to his car. He rushed to hospital, carried her in his arms and ran into the emergency room. She was gasping for air to breathe, she wasn't able to.

It had him worried about her conditions. He remained in the waiting room, and called his friend, Timothy. He was on his way. A doctor come to Kevin and provided an explanation about her condition. He sighed, "Thank God she is ok." The doctor said the baby had not been delivered yet, it may be a few hours or more. Timothy now arrived. Kevin spoke with Timothy. "Oh, God. I am sure she will be fine," he said.

Julianne screamed and screamed painfully. She sobbed heavily in a painful way, "Where the hell is Kevin? Get him now!" she said. She scratched a nurse's face madly. A nurse came running as fast as she could just to get Kevin. She ran from the private room, through to a hallway, and she was panting when she arrived at her finish line, the waiting area. She sighed. "Your woman needs you right away, so please come with me very quickly," the Nurse panted.

Kevin ran in a flash, holding her hand gently. "Take it easy, breathe easy," he said.
She exhaled, inhaling repeatedly. "Damn pain, burns like hell," she said.

"There's always pains for everyone, try to deal with it and get over it," he said.

"How could you say that? You are supposed to make me more comfortable, and in a positive state." she said.

"My bad, I am sorry. All right, let's get this done," he said.

"It is time for you to do several pushes now. Take a deep breath and push one at a time," the doctor said. She inhaled a deep breath, exhaling slowly. She pushed a hard one.

A head was on its way now. "Do several more pushes then it's over," the doctor said. Julianne pushed and pushed, the more it burned.

She cried, screaming unintelligent things. The head was coming out. She insisted on more pushes.

"Take it easy, relax, don't be hard on yourself, it's almost done. WHEW!" Kevin said. She did one very last push.

"Here we go, head's already out. You can relax now, and let us do the rest," the doctor said.

She Laughed and cried, "Finally, that damn pain is gone, but it resumes the burning," she said.

"It is normal to feel burning, and being worn out after you have delivered," the nurse said. The doctor picked up the baby, "It's a boy, congratulations!" he said. He turned him over to the nurses to do procedures on the newborn.

"What are we going to name him? Will Jeff do? What do you think?" she asked.

"We don't have any name starting with "J" in our family side at all, do we?" He asked.

"Here goes, it is Jeff we name him," she said.

The nurse carried the newborn over to Julianne, she held Jeff in her arms gently. She smiled, "Hey, you are here now, we are glad to see you, I love you," she said.

"You got strong arms, son, like mine," he smiled. He picked Jeff up, and held him in his arms softy. He kissed his forehead, with a big smile. He kissed Julianne, "I love you so much, more than anything in the world. Thank you for giving me our beautiful son," He told her tearfully.

Kevin was so excited he yelled, rushing to the waiting room to tell Timothy the rest of the news.

"Congratulations! Now you a daddy, how is she? How are you feeling about all of this?" Tim said.

"Everything goes well for both Julianne and Jeff, we named our son, Jeff," he said.

He smiled and said, "So everything looks good, but there is a concern about your son."

"What is it?" Kevin asked. "Hey you are a black cat, so will he be? Are you able to raise him in a non-violent environment and a good atmosphere?" he said.

"I have no time to think about that right now, let's worry about that later, shall we?" Kevin said.

"Okay. Let's celebrate for your son to come into the new world, and among other things, may I come see Julianne?" he asked.

"Sure, go ahead, I am sure she will be so delighted to see you," he said.

"Hey, listen, I am so proud of you. You will do great as a father should be," he smiled.

"Thanks, I needed that. Go! Go ahead and see her and the baby, I will wait here for a few moments," He cried.

Timothy went into the delivery room, and said, "Awe, she is sleeping now."

"She is sleeping due to the medicines that made her drowsy, it is for her pains. Come back in a few hours or the next day. I am sure she will be happy to see you," the nurse said.

"Sure, I will be back, please be sure to let her know that I came by to see her and the baby," he said.

"Sure, I will do that, go ahead and get some rest tonight. See you tomorrow then," the nurse said.

He headed back to the waiting room to check on Kevin. They walked toward the hallway to head to the parking lot.

"I hope everything will go well for all of us. I am worried about all the nightmares and incidents that we have been through before," Kevin said.

"Don't worry, we will find a way to deal with it, and put an end to it," Timothy said.

"I am going back home, so you should do the same. And get some rest. I will see you here tomorrow," Tim said.

"Yeah, see you then, good night, and thanks for being here for us. I appreciate it," Kevin said. They went back home. Here comes the incident in the nursery room. Jeff slept so softly, and he opened both eyes, and his eyes turned into a cat's greenish eyes. He suddenly transformed into a black cat, shrieking.

# Chapter 10

## Return of the Black Ones

Right after he denied Tiger's request, he was back into the form of a human. He got on with his life. "Got to go now, I am late for work. See you later," said Julianne.

Kevin said, "All right, shoo. Get out of here before it's too late," he laughed. He spent some time with his son, Jeff. Jeff was 2 years old. Later in the afternoon, Kevin began to feel a little shake inside his body. He thought that was just something, nothing serious.

Jeff came to his father, and asked, "Why do I have dreams?" Kevin answered his question, "That is what people have, it always will remain inside your head, it will not fade away. Why do you ask, son?" "I have dreams about a black cat, called Tiger. Is it bad dreams? I saw you in the dream, too."

He was shocked and gasped, "What? You have these dreams too? I used to have these kinds of dreams in my younger years." Kevin was thinking without saying anything. "Oh, Christ. He got it from me, like Tiger said, it will go through generation. It will never go away, it's unstoppable."

Jeff turned around from Kevin, "Please don't be afraid of me. I love you, Dad." His face was away from his father's face. Kevin didn't know what that meant. Finally, Jeff turned around toward Kevin, his body and face changed into the form of a black cat, Kevin crawled backward so quickly, frightened. It brought his memories back from his past. He thought it never would come back for his lifetime, eventually, he was wrong. Kevin was shaking again, He groaned and grunted, there was the black cat, his wife did know their history, and his history and the truth has not been revealed.

He was astonished about what just happened. He had seen that Jeff was also a cat. They went outside playing pitching. They seemed to truly enjoy all the day. Julianne got back home from work. She was deeply exhausted. She had worn herself out. She worked as a Custom Designer. She loved her job. She was about to see the truth today. Jeff and Kevin talked in private. They discussed about revealing themselves to their loved one. They agreed to show themselves to her. Julianne was cooking a dinner for the family. She was the best at cooking, better than Kevin. Kevin preferred to wait until after dinner was done. They made many riddles, jokes, teased each other during dinner, they all had so many laughs there. They finished their dinner. They cleaned the kitchen. Kevin asked Julianne to sit down at the dinner table. Jeff started the conservation.

Here came the truth. "Mom, I am a black cat," said Jeff. Julianne laughed. "Nice story, you really are funny," Julianne said. Kevin says, "He is telling the truth. It's not funny. Don't you remember what happened in the past few years?" He smiled. Julianne hardly believed it, she laughed roughly. She couldn't stop laughing.

When Julianne kept laughing, her eyes were closed. Then she opened her eyes slowly as she tried to calm herself down. Her eyes opened wide fully, and looked at Jeff and Kevin. She screamed and ran trying to find a way out of the house. Jeff ran to front door and defends it so his mother couldn't get to the door. Kevin chased Julianne off to the living room, grabbed her, trying to calm her, she continued screaming, "Get away from me, get away from me."

Kevin chuckled. "It's me, Kevin. Like I told you, I am a black cougar." Julianne shuddered, shaking, and very frightened. Along came the other black cougar, Jeff. He walked slowly toward his mother, "Don't be afraid. We will not bite and eat you alive. We are friendly cougars."

Julianne calmed down. She got up from the floor with help from Kevin and Jeff. Kevin and his son went back into human form. They smiled. "Now you see what has been going on with us? We are trying to tell you, that it is not over yet."

"We are not only both out there." Kevin explained a lot, deeply. "Oh boy, are we going to get through all of this all over again?" Julianne was stunned. It's very hard for her to deal with it and she was afraid to go through this again.

"Please do not tell anyone about this. It is between the three of us. It will keep us safe," said Kevin. Jeff hugged his mother and tried to comfort her, by singing her a song. Julianne calmed down and went to get something to drink. She had so many questions for them but she knew that they cannot answer every question. She took her chance, and asked Kevin several questions, "As you should know, we do not have all the answers to your many questions. I will tell you only what I know. That's it. You can go ahead and find out more, if you look hard and use some common sense," said Kevin.

Kevin comforted her, and put his arms around her. He held her gently, said, "I love you so much, no matter what. Do you understand?" Julianne smile was shining, "I love you too. Also, give me some time to get used to you again." They all left their home and went to some place. Kevin wanted to show his wife something, which she needed to know more of the secret.

They arrived at their cave, he took her inside the cave, where she had suffered in the past. They walked down far, long inside the cave with only two lanterns lit. There were many black cats lying down, sleeping, and snoring.

"Please be quiet, they simply can hear any sounds you are making. They don't know you, and they can be very nasty. Stay by my side," said Kevin. They found a dungeon; the one that would lead them to Tiger's chamber.

Deep inside the cave, it was very breezy, chilly, very dark. Julianne was terrified of the dark. Surprisingly, Julianne was able to handle the dark, creepy cave. Kevin told her not to worry. That she would be fine once all of them got there. It took them four hours to get to Tiger's Chamber. Julianne asked, "What happened to you? How did you become one black cat again? I thought it was all over?"

Kevin and Jeff reformed into black cats. Julianne was still shaking from fear of them, but she started to put her fear aside. Kevin explained more specifics and incidents about his pet Tiger. It saddened

Julianne. She began to understand the situation and his feelings toward his dead pet. She started to accept who they were, but in a very slow motion. It would take her time to accept the facts.

"There we go," Jeff said. They appeared at the chamber. That chamber room had three guards, two dancers, which all were Servants. They entered the chamber; Julianne was amazed by what she saw. "So, we are not alone. They're the most beautiful creatures I've ever seen," said Julianne.

"Yes. Thank you. It has been a long time," Tiger said.

"Here's your grandson, Jeff," Julianne answered. Tiger approached Jeff, and took a real look at him. They started a discussion. They agreed that Julianne was not to leak any of their secrets.

"Be sure that she does not tell anyone about this place. I do not want any disturbances," Tiger said.

"I understood as clear as crystal. I will keep eye on her," Kevin said.

"This is where we live our history for over 300 years, and continue living. This is our secret. No one will know about this place. I trust you will not tell anyone. If you do, we will have no choice but to kill you," Tiger said.

Julianne agreed. They apparently left the chamber. The trip other four hours to get outside of the Cave of Cat's Eye. Jeff made himself tough, walking all the way upstairs inside the cave. Kevin was very proud of him. They finally arrived outside of the cave. They formed back into human. Julianne drove back home. It was around nine o'clock in the evening. Jeff was very tired, worn out by the walks. He went to sleep. Kevin intended to stay up late, there were many things on his mind. Julianne took a long bath. Julianne slept in the bathtub. She looked peacefully sleeping. Kevin went into the bathroom. He walked very quiet and fingered Julianne's shoulder, to massage her. Julianne woke, gasping.

"Ooh, you scared me. What are you doing?" Julianne smiled.

"Oh, I am sorry to scare you and put you through a rough time today. This wasn't meant to happen," Kevin said. "I thought you were used to everything by now, and yet I am surprised that you are not," he said.

"Hey, Dad. I saw a black cat on my dresser, he screeched at me," Jeff said.

"What does this black cat look like?" Dad asked.

"He looks as if he has been dead, and its eyes are red," he answered.

"Oh, shit. Stay with me, don't wander off anywhere here or outside, not at all, do you understand?" Dad said. "Stay with Mom, please. I am going to check it out," he said.

He walked to his son's room. He opened the door slowly, Servants walked around very slowly, growling, looking deadly. "Shit, they are back, they are supposed to be so-so dead." He talked to himself. He closed the door very quietly. He went back to the bathroom where Julianne and Jeff were

"Sh.....they are here," Julianne said.

"What's the fuck? They are everywhere," he said. He walked backward softly, one of the Servants jumped on his shoulder from behind him, and he gasped. He turned to look at it, it shrieked. He panicked and pushed the Servant away, he fell down and bumped his head.

He woke up, groaning, trying to get up. He stood, feeling funny, there were no Servants anywhere, just a bloodstream everywhere. He ran to numerous rooms to find Julianne and Jeff, they had disappeared as well. "NO!!!!! JULIANNE" "JEFF, WHERE ARE YOU?" he screamed. He rushed to the car, and drove it off, he was speedy, arrived to see his friend, Timothy. He banged the house door, a light was turned on, Kevin could see from the windows.

The door opened, "Hey, Kevin, everything all right?" Tim asked.

"Listen, the black cats have come back; they got my wife and my son," he told him.

"What? Let me get dress up, come in," Tim sighed .

"Darkness has returned, how that is possible?" he thought. "We are going through it all over again like before. We've got to go to see Tiger, haven't we?" Kevin said.

"Yes, so it seems we have to," Tim said.

"Let's get them back, no matter what," Kevin said.

"We are going to do whatever it takes to kill them, even it costs us our lives," Tim said. They drove a long way, eventually, they arrived outside the cave. They hadn't figured out what would be the next step. Here two Servants were coming out of the cave, waiting for them to come by.

"Look at them, it's Servants, let's see what they really want," Kevin said.

# Chapter 11

## The Final Battle

Here the Servants looked at him. "You cretins gave me that look before," Kevin said. He nodded his head toward these servants, smiling. He transformed into a black cat. He pulled his sword off his back, drawing it as a defense. He walked toward the cave with two Servants out front. The Servants' were growling running in a flash, jumping straight to him. He attacked the Servants with his sword; cutting them into pieces, the Servants decomposed instantly.

Strangely, their souls came out of their bodies, as blue orbs. The blue orbs flew around at the speed of a housefly. They flew toward Kevin, and attached into his body. Kevin did not know or understand why this occurred.

"Whatever," he said. He barged into the cave. There were bloodstains on his sword, and gore. He walked through several dungeons just to start a search. He kept drawing and attacking the numerous Servants with his sword. There again, many souls came out of the bodies, and attached to him.

He felt more energy, stronger after numerous souls were attached to him. His eyes began to glow a little greenish. One of the dungeons he unexpectedly entered, "It has been a long time, son," Tiger said and smiled.

"What are you doing here? Thought you died?" Kevin said.

"The end is only the beginning, don't you think?" Tiger asked.

"You got that right. Oh well, I am going to put an end to everything, no matter what it costs," he implied. "Here we go again, this is the second battle we are doing as of right now, isn't it?" Kevin said.

Tiger drew his claws, looking very sharp more powerful than before.

"Oh, I am scared, please do not claw me," Kevin said in a mocking cry..

"Let's play the game, hey, it's an endless one, hm," Tiger said.

"Hey, don't waste my time; let's finish this for once and for all," he said.

Both ran at the same time, there were sparks spreading everywhere when there was a fight. Both were growling and screeching at each other, Kevin jumped backward, panting. He had worn himself out.

"Damn, you have gotten stronger than previously. What made you come back?" Kevin asked.

"Because everything you see here is not over as you thought it would be," Tiger said.

"Oh, really? Name one," he asked.

"You already know what I know. You ain't that good to use your knowledge, which makes you unworthy," he said. "Let's finish this one quickly."

"Where are my son and precious wife?" he asked.

"Find out yourself. You won't like what you are about to see when you have located them," Tiger said.

More growling and clanking, Kevin was on top of Tiger, Tiger got stuck kneeling on the ground with the sword drawing into his throat.

"Where are they? Tell me now. Otherwise you will wish you did," he said.

"You can't defeat me, not in any way." Tiger laughed. Screeching, Kevin slayed Tiger by his throat, the gore was everywhere. His throat was wounded openly, bleeding all over his body. "Now you see what I am made of?" Kevin said.

"Hum. You ain't that bad, you have gotten stronger, that still doesn't mean you can defeat me, anyway," he smiled. Tiger fell down to the ground, his body disappeared.

"Don't insult my ability, it isn't what you think. You have no idea what I am made of," Kevin said.

"Oh? Then show me what you are made of," Tiger said, appearing again. Kevin's hand was shaking while he held the sword. His sword had become a bluish glow; he had inherited a new ability, an unnoticeable one. He smiled, slaying Tiger in a flash. Tiger groaned and screamed, falling down on the floor completely and gasping to breathe, eventually, he failed. "Your son Jeff is down in the chamber with his mother Julianne," he said. He decomposed and disappeared. It was his last stand; he would not be resurfacing again.

He ran in search for his family, at the entrance to the chamber he eventually arrived. There were numerous Servants blocking the entrance. He thought he may have to kill them all over again. The Servants numbers continued coming. He sighed, continuing his slayings. Until the very last Servant was slayed, it happened that something dropped; a shiny white gem on the ground of the front entrance. He looked at it and picked it up. He wondered what it was for, and saw a hole on the entrance door. He decided to risk it by putting it in the hole. When he inserted it, the door cracked and opened.

As he entered the entrance of the chamber room, there was Jeff lying on the circle stone, where Kevin used to stand and transform into a black cat in the past. He panicked when he saw Julianne lying down on the ground injured outside the circle stone. He shook her to wake her up, she groaned.

"What? Where is Jeff?" she said. Jeff was right there on the ground.

"Try to get up, where are the injuries?" he asked.

"Everywhere in my body, there were a lot of cracks in my body, feels like an elephant walked on me," she said. She coughed, there was a little blood on her mouth.

Julianne got up, attempting to run to grab Jeff. Kevin stopped her, "It is his battle now, we cannot do anything, and all we can do is stand here and be there for him.," Kevin said.

"Oh God, they better not scratch him a single one, I swear to God," she said.

Jeff woke up, and tried to get up. Suddenly, he was lifted, floating in the air, unmoving.

"Hey, Jeff, listen to me, just relax, it is not harmful as long as you don't move or interfere with what is about to be done to you," Kevin said.

"I am hurt, and I am scared," Jeff said.

"I know you are, it is time to face the fear and accept what you are about to see. Just go easy on yourself," Kevin said. "Why am I floating? What are they doing to me?" Jeff asked.

"They are healing your injuries you already have and also they will present you some new abilities, you need to acquire and accept them," Kevin explained.

Jeff passed out while floating. There was light coming out of his body, it was healing him, and it took only a few minutes. He was floating down back on the floor, he got up and stood quietly, wondering around while being still. "I felt hot inside my body, I am sweating. What's going on?" Jeff asked.

"That's something you need to find out and face on your own," Kevin implied. "Here you go, be still, and see what people can't see," Kevin said.

"All right, I will try my best, without any consequences," Jeff said. There was a tall black cat standing wait for Jeff to turn his head around toward him.

"Jeff, please pay attention, look at that black cat, and listen to everything he says, very carefully," Kevin said.

Jeff now looked at that tall black cat, "Who are you?" he asked.

"My name is Raikshil, I am a guardian to this chamber, and I am here to have you inherit our abilities, among other things. Please listen carefully and make the right choices, do you understand?" Raikshil said. "You were born by a human and a black cat, as you were born; you were transformed into a black cat. You carry your father's blood and mother's. You will have great difficulty to deal with the future, just like your father. Most important, you will go through what your father has. So, here goes, let's begin, and please remember there is no harm," he said.

"Okay, let's do this," Jeff said. Raikshil faded and disappeared. Jeff looked at his parents, he turned his head to the other side, the process of transformation was completed, and he became a black cat as he turned around to the side and looked toward his parents. "Is this what I have to face and accept?" Jeff asked.

"Yes, but remember, it is your choice to make, not ours," Kevin said. He smiled, and his body now shook, there was something glimmering and floating toward Jeff. It was a blue liquid sword, a new one for a young one. Jeff grabbed it, the sword was lightweight and when it was grabbed, the light inside the sword become more brighter, then it faded out. He hold the sword in his hand, looking at it real good, "Wow, this is such an awesome sword," he smiled.

Raikshil reappeared, "Are you ready to accept what you have already seen? Will you be able to face the gruesome events in future?" he asked.

"Yes, I think I am. Why has this happened to me and others? What causes all of this?" Jeff asked.

"It is not time for you to understand, because you are so young, it takes time to learn and see the truth." Raikshil said.

"Okay, I understand. When can I see you again?" Jeff asked.

"You will, someday. Meanwhile, go back to your parents now and live normal," Raikshil said.

He again faded out, Jeff transformed back into human form. He ran to his parents happily. "Let's get out of here, this place creep me out," Jeff said. They all three smiled, they walked out of the cave, it was a bright day.

"Dad, will we have nightmares again?" he asked.

"The nightmares are endless, nothing can stop the nightmares," Kevin said. They all walked back to the car, and took a ride back home.

# Chapter 12

## End of the Nightmares

Here came the most riveting nightmares Kevin and Jeff were having. After the incident at the chamber, Kevin began to have gruesome nightmares. That night, he was sweating and making many movements, while he was asleep. It disturbed Julianne, it woke her up and she pushed Kevin repeatedly. "Damn, why can't you just wake up?" She said. Kevin slept like a stone. Meanwhile, he woke up inside one of his nightmares.

He was inside his house, he saw Julianne was sleeping, so was Jeff. He didn't realize that he was inside his dream. He walked to his foyer, near the living room; he stopped so quickly when he saw a Servant with reddish glowing eyes standing glaring at him. "Shoo, shoo, go away, I am not going to deal with you," he said. The Servant began to walk slowly, and it dissolved and decomposed very slowly. It snarled angrily, it faded away and reappeared in a small area. Kevin was trying to locate the Servant. After a few attempts, he found it and had it cornered. "You should not have come back," he said. He transformed into a black cat, and drew his sword. He slay it by cutting through its head, it decomposed too quickly. He smiled, and attempted to walk back to the foyer, as he turned around toward the living room, he gasped; there were so many Servants, screaming and screeching, even snarling. They took a step toward him then jumped straight to him. Kevin closed his eyes in fear.

Kevin woke up screaming from his nightmare, "Are you all right? I tried to wake you up, you slept like the dead," she said.

"Damn those nightmares," he panted.

"Where is Jeff? Is he all right?" he asked.

"Yes, he is fine, still asleep as well," she said.

"I don't know why this has been going on, I thought it was over," he said.

"Well, like you said, nightmares are endless, nothing will go, will it?" she said. Kevin went to the kitchen to get something to drink.

Julianne went back to sleep. Kevin went to check on Jeff, in his bedroom. He saw a black cat sitting next to him. It growled softly, as though it was very angry to see Kevin. He kept it to himself, without causing any scenes. He wouldn't want to put Jeff through what he has been through before. He then left his room, headed back to his bedroom. He lay back on the bed and turned the television on. His eyes began to doze off, a few minutes later; he fell asleep with the television left on.

The odor bothered Kevin while he was sleeping. He rubbed his nose and had his hand covering his nose. It did not help, He was puzzled, yawning he got up by bending while lying on the bed. He felt something heavy on his legs, he was trying to move his legs around to make himself comfortable but he still felt the discomfort. He turned on a lamp; and found a dead black cat lying on his legs. He picked it up by its tail, and stared at its head with its eyes open and his mouth open wide. He stared at it for few moments, it was a scary moment; its head was upside down, it moved up and growled. He screamed and threw it against the wall. He leapt out of the bed, and checked for the body of the black cat where he threw it, the body was completely disappeared.

"Damn. I am tired of this shit. I gotta check on Jeff," he said. He went out to his room, and checked on him. From what he saw, he was sleeping very well, but Kevin noticed that he was sweating lightly, like with a sleep disorder. He knew not to disturb his sleep. He left his room and headed back to his bedroom, tucking himself into bed. A few hours later, the hallway was lit, it caused a great disturbance of Kevin's sleep. He was very tired, he could hardly wake up, he jumped out of bed, to see what was going on. There was Jeff walking down the hallway, with his eyes closed.

"I see that he is sleepwalking. Let's see what he is up to," He thought. He followed Jeff very quietly. Jeff made it into the living room, toward the coffee table. He picked up something, and petted it. Kevin watched him doing it, he didn't see anything visible. The rotten odor started to appear. He sniffed, he knew something wrong was coming. He took a few steps toward Jeff very gently, when he got close to Jeff, something in his arms started to show itself. A black cat appeared in his arms, his eyes remaining closed. Its growled, screeched, and suddenly it jumped at Kevin in an angry way. He attempted to hit and shovel the black cat, the attack failed, because the black cat was fading away before being hit.

Jeff fell down while he was sleeping, he was sweating heavily, he was wet from sweat all over. Kevin came to him, and carried him to his bedroom, put him down and tucked him into bed. He intended to sleep on the floor near his son for these reasons. In the morning, Kevin stretched and went to check on Julianne, He knew Jeff was already up. Julianne was still sleeping, he smiled, and gave her a kiss on her cheek. She sighed and smiled while sleeping beautifully.

"I had a strange dream last night, what happened to me? Why was I sweating so much?" Jeff asked.

"Yes, you were sleepwalking and petted one of the black cats for a while," he said.

"What do you mean, I was sleepwalking? What does it mean?" his son questioned.

"It means you were walking in your sleep, and you were doing things that you either do not remember or did not realize that you had done," he said.

"Is it bad? Have you ever had one?" he asked again.

"Yes, I had these too many times, it is not necessarily bad, it is common for everyone, and they do have these issues. There is really nothing wrong with it," he explained.

"My body started to sweat and burn, it hurt sometimes, I wanted it to stop," Jeff said.

"These symptoms you are having, they affect the nightmares, and possibly the transformation," he said. They wished that the nightmares they currently had could be stopped or got rid of. They were trying to work on this main issue. They believed that the nightmares could be stopped, or treated. Actually, there was absolutely nothing that could stop the recurring dreams or nightmares, but it could be treated itself, by controlling it.

They thought that their nightmares had to be either attempted to be rid of, or ended. They didn't realize that nightmares are still there inside their head. "End of the Nightmares" wasn't totally true.

# Chapter 13

## The Resurrected of the Black Ones

After they have thought to end their nightmares, their thoughts turned out to be very wrong. Later at night, there was a very serious incident which was very unusual, a strange phase. They now smelled a very strong odor, like rotten eggs. "What the hell is that smell? It makes me gag," she said.

"I don't know yet. Let's get calm; I will go check that out," Kevin said.

As Kevin walked to the window to look outside, he gasped. "Oh, shit. I see several Servants outside walking toward our place. Both of you go lock all the windows and make sure the are doors secured," Kevin said.

"Why is that?" Jeff asked. "We are going to have problems right now," Kevin said. They all three already secured their place. They even turned off all the lights, except Jeff's television.

Julianne caught two Servants sitting by the kitchen window, watching her gruesomely. She screamed, panicked, and ran to Kevin. "There are cats at the kitchen window," she said. Kevin rushed into the kitchen. There was nothing. He went to the window again. There were more and more Servants coming up. They had their building surrounded. Strangely, there were no people, except these three and the Servants.

Jeff walked gently to his bedroom, to get his favorite doll, the one that made him feel safe. At the time he entered his bedroom, there was many dead cats all over the place, looking like there had been a bloodbath. He shuddered, closing the door softly, and once he succeeded in closing the door, he ran as fast as he could. There were the sounds of cracks and bangs on his door. The door was cracked and it exploded, without a fire. Hundreds of Servants overflowed through the door, alive.

Kevin could feel a heavy vibration, as if the floor was about to collapse, but it wouldn't collapse. He jumped across the sofa and bumped into Jeff while he was running.

"Stay with Mom," Kevin said. He could sense that the Servants were in the hallway. When he ran into the hallway, they were there quietly sitting, glaring at him, then they disappeared, and left a large amount of bloodstains. It confused him, how they got in, and then suddenly disappeared.

The Servants kept coming. They all three looked outside the window, there were more than a hundred dozen Servants around the building. "What are we going to do? There are numerous Servants surrounding us, how can we get rid of them?" Julianne asked.

"I have absolutely no idea of how to get rid of them," he said.

"Let's wait and see, and I will think of something else. Oh hey, what about Timothy? We have not heard or seen him for such a long time, have we?" he said.

"Let me see if I can get hold of him," Julianne said.

"Why does this keep happening to us? What have we done?" Jeff asked.

"They just do, no apparent reasons at the moment. We will find out more at a later time," Kevin said.

"Oh, my God. They are now walking toward the building, a few of them are already up at the windows below," Julianne said.

"Are you kidding? How bad is it?" Jeff asked.

"There are way too many of them coming up. Looks like they are going to break in the windows," she said.

"Don't transform yourself, just not yet. Wait for my signal, got it?" Kevin said.

"All right, got it, Dad," Jeff said. They finally broke into the windows on all sides of the building. They entered at normal speed, they were not in a rush. Kevin felt he was unable to battle them all at once, since there were so numerous, outnumbering him.

"Have you got hold of Timothy yet?" he asked.

"No luck. I hope he is all right. How far is he from here? Are we able to get to him?" Julianne asked.

"I doubt it, because there are too many, we are stuck here by ourselves," he said.

From the view of building, Servants were climbing halfway up the building, and already there were numerous ones inside the building. They kept coming up, nothing could stop them. "I better get going, I will do my best to clear up some floors down here. I will see what our defense will most likely be," Kevin said. "Like I said, don't do anything until I give you a signal or something. Just stay with Mom," Kevin said.

"Please be careful. Don't get hurt, please. I am a little scared," Jeff said.

"Just watch out for any kind of signal," Kevin said. Jeff sat down on the sofa with his mother to calm down. "See you in a little bit," Kevin told them. Kevin left the apartment and locked the door. He transformed into a black cat. He took out his sword and drew it in a defensive way. He checked the floor where he was at present, they were clear, no presence. He took a stair down to the next floor. He had encountered a few Servants. He normally smiled every time he was started a mini-battle. He ran screaming and growling, killing several of them.

"None of you are going to get my precious son and wife, if you intend to get them, you have to get over my dead body first," he talked to himself. He moved himself to the next floor down after he completed the first two floors. It was the third floor he had to clear up now. There was 13 Servants standing in a formal line, waiting for him. "You gotta be kidding; you think you can wipe me out?" Kevin laughed.

He walked toward them, they became decomposed cats. They ran and jumped at him, while they jumped, they dissolved and faded away. Kevin stood quietly, without any hesitation. It looked like it was getting easier for him, he had gotten used to it. In what way, he did not know, because he had not mastered his ability yet. He cleared up a few more floors with killing, bloodshed. He had not been injured in any way. His reaction was very calm, no panic, and no rages.

He had completely cleared out most of the floors. "I hope Dad is okay, it has been a while now. He has not returned," Jeff said. "I am not worried about it because I know he will be fine. He is trying to stop whatever is coming to us. Let's check outside through the windows to see anything new," she said. They walked up to the window, the Servants were past halfway, climbing up the building. "Let's back away, they are coming," she said. She went to close the curtains by the kitchen window, among other windows.

"We'll stay up against the wall, for our safety. Don't scream, or do anything funny unless it is necessary," she said.

"Will we be all right? How do I know if my dad gives me a signal, since the curtains are closed?" Jeff asked.

"You will know, trust me, you will," she said. Kevin succeeded in stepping onto the final floor, he rested for a few minutes, getting ready for the big battle coming.

"Will Jeff be able to help me with this battle? Is he ready?" Kevin mumbled to himself.

"Mom, I can feel the burning starting inside of me. I am not sure if I can hold it down until Dad needs me," Jeff said.

"Just wait a bit more, do not let it out yet," she said. Kevin came to the front door, there was a small window on the door, and he could see the overflow of Servants outside.

"It is time for me to give my son a signal, I am sure I need his help," Kevin said to himself. He kicked and smashed the front door, and screamed. He ran into them, slaying them with his sword, he continued slaying them. There was shrieking and growling, the Servants had become very angry.

The building was shaking lightly. "It is time for me, that's the signal he is sending for me," Jeff said. "I am sorry, I have to do this, and I have to help my dad at any cost," he said.

"Just be careful, don't put yourself into any harmful way, go for it, and show your dad what you are made of," she said.

"See you later, I love you, Mom," he said. He could feel the burning more and more, he was ready to be transformed into a cat. Eventually, he transformed himself into one, and carried a very powerful blue sword. He walked up to the window, opened the curtain, and found his dad fighting them off. "Wish me the best. I've got to get going," Jeff said. Julianne was trying to get a hold of Timothy.

Jeff ran and jumped, breaking through the window and screaming. He landed on the ground, cracking the ground. "Here I am. Let's finish this the best we can," Jeff said. "You ready? Try not to get yourself killed. I know you will do better than I do. Go for it," Kevin said.

# Chapter 14

## Chronicles of Battle

Jeff and Kevin stood very closely together, surrounded by Servants around them. They continued fighting their best. Most of the Servants were fighting with them, but some just decomposed and disappeared. Kevin did not know why this occurred.

"We gotta split up, the more we can finish them off," Kevin said.

Jeff sighed, running and trying to get through them by bumping into them and killing them. Kevin continued slaying them as much as he possibly could.

"Damn, they are too much for me and Jeff. We are only two here, no one else," Kevin said to himself. Jeff kept up what he was doing.

"I ought to get to the car and drive it to get to Dad," Jeff was thinking.

Julianne saw both of them fighting them unstoppably. She still could not reach Timothy. The Servants were currently climbing the building, close to getting into the kitchen window and the balcony. She took a risk by running out of the apartment, and down to the front door. Meanwhile, as she was running, there were some encounters surprising her. She had no weapons, but used her legs as a weapon by kicking them.

She was scared as hell, but being a tough lady, continued fighting them to get through to the front door. She was injured, with some scratches, and bad cuts. Kevin saw her coming out of the front door with all that blood.

"Are you all right? Where's Jeff?" he asked.

"I saw him running to the car while fighting them," she said.

"Stay there at the front door, until Jeff gets back," he said.

Jeff made it inside the car. He had a lot of blood over him from slaying the cats. He happened to have a car key.

"Let's get my dad and mom; I am going to skewer the cats by driving over them," he talked to himself. He started the car, and put it in driving gear, he pedaled fully. He smashed many Servants while driving. Accidentally, he hit the building, but the damage was only minor. He got out of the car and ran to get Julianne and Kevin.

Two Servants jumped on Kevin's back, "Damn you, get off my dad, you cretins," Jeff said. He jumped high and attacked these two Servants, and killed them.

"Thanks, son. Where's the car?" he asked.

"It's right there by the front door, where's Mom?" Jeff asked.

"She is inside by the front door, waiting for you. Go get her; I will meet you at the car," Kevin said.

Jeff cooperated, and went inside the building; found his mom sat on the floor injured. He got her up, and put her arms around his shoulder, and helped her walk down the door to get to the car.

"Where's Dad? Is he still fighting?" she asked.

"Yes, he's still fighting, he said he will meet us at the car. So, let's get there, shall we?" he said.

These two walked out of the building, with all of the Servants still wandering. They rushed into the car; he put his mom in the back of the car. Kevin got in the driver's side. Jeff ran around the car to get to the passenger's side, and got in.

Servants jumped and got on the car – many of them. Kevin was not able to see the view; he turned on to wipe them out. To wipe, not only wipe them out well. Kevin went on driving, without any view. Jeff used his sword to kill the Servants and get rid of those on the windshield. Thousands of Servants chased them off. Now Kevin finally has a clear view to drive. He sped into Route 70, a highway. There was no one or any vehicles on Interstate 70; the way it looked did not make sense.

The servants continued chasing unstoppably. Kevin began to lose the control of driving. The fuel was running out, Kevin looked back and saw Servants chasing them, as he turned his head back to the front of the driving, there was another group of Servants running toward him. He drove roughly when he was trying to make a turn. The car rolled and crashed, luckily Jeff and Julianne had themselves belted in. Kevin didn't have his belt on. He fell out of the front window, flying, he smashed into the road, in a condition of serious injuries.

The Servants were making a heavy crowd around them inside the circle. Kevin was currently in the form of the black cat, Jeff returned to his human form . Jeff came out of the car with minor injuries. Julianne had the same conditions, only had a serious cut and bleeding on her forehead. Kevin was in a very delicate condition. He could not get up, he was too weak to make any kind of response at the moment. They were shocked, utterly upset by what they saw in Kevin.

The crowd of Servants shrunk, the more it shrank, they all three surrendered, and had no way out of the crowd.

Timothy drove down the highway, not realizing what was going on. Until he got a big view of the crowd, he was shocked, and got out of the car, standing, and looking for them. He felt it was necessary to drive through, he went for it, and skewered numerous Servants, and found Kevin lying down on the road with Julianne and Jeff crying over him, trying to wake him up.

Timothy ran in a panic, Servants shrieking at him, he ignored them. "What happened? What's going on? I have got your calls, but the signals are dead here." Timothy asked.

"Damn those black cats, they kept coming at my building, and it has gotten worse, and it drained Kevin's energy and his strength. We tried to escape them, it was a failure," Julianne cried.

"Is Dad going to die? Please wake him up," Jeff sobbed.

Kevin groaned and sighed. "You got here on time, we have been trying to get a hold of you, and we came to get you and your help," Kevin said.

"Don't talk, just stay down, you are in a bad shape, so do not move," Timothy said.

"It is too late. Nothing you guys can do about it," Kevin said.

"No, you are not going to die, are you?" Jeff asked.

"I am sorry that you have to see me this way," Kevin said. Kevin formed into a black cat again. "Here's my sword, please take it with you," he said. Jeff came to him, and took the sword out of his hand.

"What am I supposed to do with this? Tell me," Jeff asked.

"You take it with you. You need to wield it within you," Kevin said.

Jeff was sobbing, and sitting on his knees and holding Kevin's hand tightly. He lay his head on his chest, arm around him, hugging him tightly. "Son, I love you more than anything in the world. But, listen, you need to be brave, and keep going on, no matter what. You need to take care of your mother as well. Don't let anyone take away everything from you that you already have. I know this, in my heart, you will be master, and defeat those powerful Servants." He gasped for air. "You now have two swords in your hands. Do not lose them; you need those more than anything to defend yourself and your family. Do you understand?" Kevin asked.

"Yes, I do. I will finish them off, and finish what you have started, at any cost," Jeff said.

"You are such a good boy, please take care of your mom, you hear me?" I am sorry to tell you this now, I have to go now, goodbye, my precious," Kevin said. His pupils expanded full of black, he gasped for the air, trying to breath, and he failed, and his eyes closed. His breath stopped. Julianne and Jeff sobbed heavily. Timothy had a good cry, holding his hand tightly. "I will take care of them, I promise," he said.

Jeff got up and put his two swords into his back blade pocket. "I am going to finish you all off for good," he said. He screamed angrily, transforming into a black cat and screeching, growling quietly. "My dad has done the chronicles of battle for years; I am going to finish everything for him. No one will stop me, not even either of you," Jeff said angrily.

# Chapter 15

## Upcoming Souls

After Jeff's outburst of his anger, he fell down on his knees. "What am I going to do without him gone? Nothing turned out good without him around," he cried. The crowd of Servants backed away a little, slowly. Timothy went to get Jeff up, he pulled him up, "I am sorry that your dad died, but you still have got to be brave, he would have wanted you to do that for him," he said.

They both stood, Timothy gave him a hug. He glared at his dad's body, "Oh, boy. He's standing and looking well, He's a ghost, isn't he?" Timothy said.

"What do you mean? Dad's alive?" he asked.

"Turn around and look at him. Tell me what you see?" Timothy asked.

Jeff turned around, "DAD! I thought you died?" Jeff said.

"Hey, son. Come to me, now. I want to show you something." he said. Jeff dropped his swords on the ground, and ran to his father. "Look around you, tell me what you see?" Kevin asked.

"I see all Servants around us, they scared me, why are they still here?" he implied.

"They are still here because they won't let this get over if they want something from us, they would have gone if I have died, but they didn't. It means you have something they want. Do not give them anything at all, even if you don't know what it is, all you gotta do is to keep fighting and running, no matter what. The reason is that you are not ready for this. You will know when you are ready," Kevin said. "Do not be afraid of anything that will come to you, you need to confront them, and fight them for what you believe in. Like I said, at any cost," Kevin said.

"I know I'll never forget everything you have told me, and what you have taught me. What will the sword you gave me do for me?" Jeff asked.

"Use it very wisely, the more ability you will learn, it will make you stronger than you are now," Kevin said. "Never let anyone got a sight of this sword, I think they want this, among other things," Kevin said.

"I won't let anyone take this away from me, ever. I promise," Jeff said.

"Good, I am counting on you. Now, you gotta see something, which will help you understand," Kevin said.

Thousands of souls appeared in blue streams, walking toward Kevin and Jeff. Julianne and Timothy was shocked,

"I have never seen real ghosts in my entire life, have you?" Timothy said.

"No, I never saw one. It's so beautiful," Julianne said. The souls that appeared in blue, it seems were black cats who used to be in human form. Seven of the souls came to Jeff, "We will take care of your father, Kevin. He has been through suffering for years, it is time to end his suffering," said one of the souls.

"Will he be there for me anywhere, anytime I need him?" Jeff asked.

"Of course, yes, he will always be here for you, even inside your heart. He loved you so much more than you would know," said one of the souls.

One of the souls came to Jeff, and explained to him. "I am Kaithi, please bring me your father's sword, and I will show you something that I want to pass on to you," said Kaithi. Jeff went and got the sword, and brought it to her. "Hold the sword gently, and listen and watch it. You will see a burst of light come into it. We, all the souls who have carried this sword, would like to be your strength. We souls will become orbs and that will go inside your sword. Do not be afraid.

Hold the sword still. You will know when it is done and can put it away," Kaithi said.

"Okay, here we go. It's heavy, but I can hold it a bit longer," Jeff said. Kaithi became a blue orb, and flew into the sword, then all the souls that were by Jeff's side became orbs, and flew into the sword in a flash.

The sword Jeff held onto became a very bluish bright light. Then it faded away. Jeff didn't feel that sword was heavy anymore; he was able to hold it and carry it. Jeff looked around and noticed that all the Servants had decomposed, and fallen down the ground, as if they were dying. He went to his father, but he had disappeared. His body remained lying on the road. Julianne and Timothy went to him, and patted his back, Julianne hugging him tightly. Jeff wasn't responsive to it. Once all the souls had faded away, the Servants had not disappeared yet, their bodies remained on the ground, visible.

"What will we do next? Are you guys going to help me?" Jeff asked.

"I think you know what to do, and we will stand by you, in any way. We will be here if you need us," Timothy said. Julianne joined to agree with what Timothy said to him.

"We gotta take his body somewhere, to bury him properly," Julianne said.

"Where do you think we should bury him?" Timothy asked.

"I think we should bury him right where he almost died before. Near the Cave of Cat's eye, don't you think?" Julianne said.

"Yes, let's take him there before something gets worse," Timothy said. "Let's go to my car, since your car has been wrecked," Timothy added.

"Be careful with his body, I don't want him scratched, not at all," Jeff said.

"Got it. We will make sure that he has been taken care of. Go in the car, and rest," Timothy said. Jeff walked to the car, his eyes became like a cat's then it faded. Timothy picked up and carried Kevin's body to the car, Julianne held him gently in the back of the car. Jeff sat in the front of the car with Timothy.

They drove a few hours to the spot where they agreed to bury him. Jeff took a good rest. He slept smoothly. Julianne was crying softly when she looked at Kevin, he had gone back to human form.

"I love you, I will always miss you, and I will always be here for you," Julianne said in tears. She fell asleep on Kevin's chest near his head. She held him tightly. Timothy cried lightly, he had thoughts of the good memories he had with Kevin.

Jeff snored loudly, with his two swords in his arms. Eventually, the swords faded away when he was back in human form. The swords would always be there when he was back in the form of a black cat. Timothy had not realized, he was focused on driving, in a haywire way. After they drove away from the scene, all the Servants has been resurrected, following them unnoticeably.

They arrived the place. Timothy woke them both up, "We are here now; let's get this done before the sunset," he said. Timothy went to the back door and helped carry Kevin out of the car with the help of Julianne. There was already a big hole down in the ground. "That's where we should put him in; there is a shovel in his trunk. I'll go get the shovel, I'll do the filling up. You guys rest, there is some food in the car, I am sure that you both are hungry," Timothy said. He put Kevin's body in the hole gently, softly, in a proper pattern.

Jeff watched Timothy's whole work, He resumed his tears, but had good thoughts of his father. "Here's some food, go ahead and eat. You look hungry as well as I am," Julianne said. Jeff chewed some food.

"Will we not see him ever again? Will he really be here when I really need him so desperately?" Jeff asked.

"No matter where you are, he will always be there with you, and in your heart," Julianne said.

Timothy was now filling up the hole. Jeff saw a bright light blinking on Kevin's neck. "Hey, hold on, I saw something down there. I am going to it," Jeff said. Jeff jumped in the hole, and looked for something that was a blinking light, he found it was a pendant, he took it off him, there was a stone on the pendant, blinking brightly in the light . The light was gone when he held the pendant in his hand.

He put the pendant on his neck. It started to light flashing in blue. Jeff was shaking, his whole body, he felt burning inside him. It made his anger even more raging. His anger had grown like his father's. He jumped out of the hole angry, and landed on the ground.

"Finish filling up the hole now, please," Jeff nastily said. Jeff suddenly became very raging, transforming into a black one. He screamed loudly, sounding angry. Timothy and Julianne had to cover their ears with their hands.

"You guys stay away from me, just for a while. I have to take care of this, and am going to finish this off, you guys go somewhere you will be safe. I have to do this alone," Jeff said. Jeff suddenly disappeared like with a whoop.

"He disappeared, how can he do that? We've got to find him," Julianne said.

"No, we are not going to find him, let him go; this is his fight, not ours. Trust me, he will come out fine," Timothy said.

# Chapter 16

## Son's Angers

Julianne and Timothy finished burying Kevin. They left in the car and drove to Timothy's place. "Let's rest while we can. I am sure Jeff will be fine. Let's not worry too much," he said.

"Thanks for being there for us, helping us. I appreciate that," she said.

"Let's get some sleep, give me a holler if you need me," he said.

"Alright, good night. Take Care. See you in the morning," she said.

According to Jeff, he disappeared on the highway 70, he found the crowd of the Servants, well alive. He drew one of his swords, not the one belonging to Kevin. He was very quiet; his rage had been growing and growing. His eyes has became a greenish glow, the anger in him was about to burst. Half of the crowd had found him stalking them. They turned around and walked back straight to Jeff. "Come on, you killed my father, big mistake," he thought.

He bent his legs in a jump, but stayed on the ground, he held his sword up and was prepared for the battle. As Servants started to run readily to attack him. He ran and faded away repeatedly while running. When they all get much closer, he shrieked, growling loudly. He had started the bloodshed, his anger made him stronger, to avenge for his father's death.

More Servants were coming, even if most of them had been slashed. Jeff had not been worn out, there was plenty of energy inside him. He continued slashing those Servants, nothing could stop him, he was in such an unbreakable shape. Servants had gotten him with scratches, and bites, claws. He had no reaction to these kinds of attacks; anger caused no feelings, or he was feeling very numb.

The battle continued all night, and next half day, Julianne went to make breakfast, and Timothy cleaned out of his car. They both had been wondering what Jeff was up to. They had not heard from him since last night. "Don't you think we should just check on him, to be sure if he is okay? Will he be so angry at us for doing this?" Julianne asked.

"He might be angry at us, He might be happy to see us at the same time he is angry with us," Timothy said.

"Should we risk it? I think we should," Julianne said.

"I guess we have no choice, but go to find him," he said. They tucked themselves into the car, and drove. They felt funny not seeing any people around at all, so very quiet around the town as if it had been dead for decades.

As soon as they got on Interstate 70, they started to see piles of dead Servants there. "That must be Jeff's doing, all of these piles, doesn't it?" Timothy said.

"I believe he has done this, I am surprised he is able to handle this alone at the amount of Servants being killed," she said. Timothy insisted on keeping driving until they found him. A few miles later, they happily found him, he was still fighting with them.

Timothy drove through them, to kill Servants, and help Jeff be able to finish them off. "What have I told you? Didn't I?" Jeff said.

"You just don't know how to ask for help; you never admitted you need help, do you?" Julianne said.

"Ugh. Damn you. All right. Let's skewer them real good," he said.

He fell down on the road. His body was burning more, and his shape started to grow. He screamed painfully. Timothy was still driving and smashing more servants. Jeff just burst and was lifted into the air. He grew bigger, and very much stronger, he drew his father's sword, the light had gotten very bright. He closed his eyes for a few minutes, then suddenly he woke up, flying like a hummingbird into the sky, he fell down with his head downside; he closed his eyes, and was very quiet.

"He can fly? He looked very different what is he trying to do?" Julianne asked.

"We have no idea, but let's see what is going to happen," he said. As nearer the ground he fell down, he opened his eyes and his eyes became bluish like his father's. Here, he switched his side to upside and landed on the ground pretty hard and slashed his sword into the ground. There was an "electric" looking flash that exploded into the crowd, the servants started to decompose and melt.

There were so many loud sounds of screeches and shrieks from the crowd of servants. They were fading away. They kept screaming painfully. Jeff opened his eyes with a bluish glow, looking at Julianne and Timothy. He stood up and pulled the sword out of the ground. All the servants were gone, fallen down on the ground, and became ashes. The sword disappeared, he still carried one of his own swords.

He went back into human form; fell down, no response, unconscious . Julianne ran to him, grabbed him before he hit the ground. "Hey, Jeff, wake up, please wake up," she said. Jeff did not respond at all. He closed his eyes, seemingly resting. "We better take him in, and take him home, let him rest."

"He has had a very rough day since yesterday with his father's death; let's cut him a big slack, shall we?" Timothy said.

They took him home, put him in his bed, he looked very restful, and still not responding in any kind of way. Julianne and Timothy went back to the living room, sitting on the sofa, "I need some nap, and can I sleep on your lap?" Julianne asked.

"Sure, go ahead. I don't mind," Timothy said.

"Thanks, and let me know when Jeff is up," Julianne said. She fell asleep. Timothy looked at her, he felt very badly for her, because of her loss of her husband that she loved the utmost.

Timothy fell asleep and dozed off on the sofa as well. They all finally had a very good sleep. They shut their eyes heavy, like a stone. There were no nightmares recurring, only they thought of Kevin. They all three cried during their sleep. Next morning, Jeff jumped out of the bed, ran to his mother, patting her, to wake her up.

"Hey, mom, is everything ok? What happened? How did I get here?" Jeff asked.

"Don't you remember what happened yesterday?" she asked.

"Not all of it, all I remember that I went crazy with rage and disappeared when I was a black cat. Then I woke up in my bedroom," he said.

"Give it time; you will start to remember everything. Just have patience," Timothy said.

# Chapter 17

## Return to the Cave

Several days later, he sat on his bed; his memory lane had come back in parts. He remembered most of the incidents. "Am I having the abilities my dad passed on to me? Am I a being more powerful than my dad was?" he mumbled. He kept it to himself and was quiet and had a good few tears.

"How are you? Are you feeling all right?" Julianne asked. "Yes, I feel much better now, but there is something that actually bothers me. I don't know what it is," he said.

"I am sorry about what happened and it was such an unexpected event for all of us," she said.

"I was thinking of visiting that cave again, there is something we either missed or overlooked," Jeff told her.

"I don't think so; the cave collapsed after the events with your father," she answered.

"Well, yes, it has collapsed, but all of the cave? I don't think so. We better get there as soon as possible. There has to be a way to get inside the cave, I am going to see if there is what I really need," he said. "I have a gut feeling that there is something wrong down there, something bad is going to happen to us," he said.

"Will it make you feel better if we go there? To find what you think you need? Will that be helpful?" Timothy asked.

"Definitely it will, I will appreciate it very much if you guys join with me to go there. Will you guys?" Jeff asked.

"Sure, like we told you, we are here whenever you need us. Let's get ready, and head out there," Julianne said. "I am afraid that there might be more violence? Can you handle all of that? I don't want to see you get hurt or killed if you are not ready for it. Do you understand?" Julianne said.

"Hey, if there is a battle, it is between them and me, not either of you. It is mine," Jeff said.

"I got it as clear as crystal. Let's get going," Timothy said. They burst into the car, and drove off on the highway. It was only another few hours of driving for them, they are beginning to hate the long drive, actually, it annoyed them pretty much frequently now.

As they neared the cave, there was a very strong odor again, the worse than the one they have sniffed before. They were about 4 or 5 miles away from the cave.

"We are near there, I could sense it, and even I could smell the dead out there," Jeff said. They were close to the last exit to the cave. Timothy was driving at the normal speed, it was unexpected for him. The windshield cracked all of a sudden, it caused Timothy to lose his control over the drive, he braked and drove over the shoulder into the ground, luckily there was no damage to the car at that moment.

"What the hell was that?" Timothy said. Julianne got out of the car and looked around the front to see what had smashed the windshield.

"Oh, shit. It was a black cat; they know we are coming, don't they?" she asked.

"I have no idea, but that would be an idea. Just throw the black cat away, so we can get on the road," Timothy said.

She picked up the black cat, it was cold and hard as rock. While she was attempting to throw it away, she looked at its face, screeching, it resumed its life, it tried to escape from her hand. It shook, moving roughly then it dissolved in a gory way. She screamed and threw it away, she ran panicking into the car. They drove through the woods, the very same trail they used before. As they neared the cave, a few Servants were seen, which Jeff saw but he didn't say one word; he knew there would be a battlefield inside the cave. He stayed positive, become very confident.

Here goes, they were walking and arrived at the outside entrance of the collapsed cave. "Let's find a way to get in, let me know what you find," Jeff said.

"Do you want us to come with you to go inside?" both asked.

"No, not at the moment, I will go in myself, remember, I have to do this alone," Jeff said. A little while later, Jeff found a way, giving Julianne a holler.

"Found it? Too easy, is it?" she said.

"Yup, it is to me." "Well, I guess it is time for me. See you whenever I am done," he said. He turned into a black cat. He went inside, somehow the stones were loose and fell down through the hole. He fell down to the ground. He groaned and exhaled. "Damn, my butt hurts, ouch," he said. "Hush, what's next? Where am I supposed to go?" he said to himself.

There were three tunnels; he decided to go through the first left tunnel. He would attend to the other two after going through the first one. It was very dark, but black cats have night vision; he would not have any problems with his visions, he walked very quietly and being very defensive. He entered the tunnel; very few Servants were there unnoticeable until he walked closer, their eyes turned reddish glow. Snarling and screaming, they jumped on him, he grabbed two by his hands, and squeezed the life out of them.

The Servants were thrown on the ground, unmovable, definitely dead. He laughed lightly, resuming his walking line. There was blue fire nearby, he prepared and drew his sword.

"Woo. Let's get this over with." he said. He apparently arrived into the room with blue fire torches hanging on the wall. There was basically nothing there. He didn't think he needed to check it out, he turned back to the entrance of the tunnel. As soon as he walked into the tunnel, there was a strong wind and it blew out the blue fire. He froze, very quiet, and turned looking around.

One step more he took. There were lights flashing like an x-strobe, dozens of Servants appeared, into human-like black cats. They marched toward him; Jeff bent his knee a little and moved and held the sword up. He snickered softly, "I am going to smooch them bloody," he said to himself. "COME THE TIME!!" he said. He ran into the crowd, gutsy, the Servants had their weapons. Clanging and slinging his swords, he screamed angrily. "Do me more, come on, you gutless losers!!" he said.

Julianne and Timothy had a long conservation at the outside sitting on the car's hood. They looked worry-free, very positive. "Whew! Damn stink, it's rotten coming from the cave, isn't it?" Julianne said.

"Yeah, I think it is. We can walk a little farther to get fresh air," he said. They walked a few blocks away from the cave. They sighed and panted from walking. They felt comfortable at that spot now.

Jeff completed the mini-battle in the first area. He had minor scratches, not bleeding. He walked out of the first tunnel, he sat down, ripping a small cloth and wrapped it on his left lower arm. He rested, thinking what to do next, without any hesitation. He stood up and stretched himself, sighing. He now entered the second tunnel, the middle one. "Hope it is not as bad as the last one," he said.

When he attempted to walk into the tunnel – the wind blew very strong, he insisted to continue trying to enter. Which he succeeded finally, entering the huge room, with no fire torches. Something was much different in the room. There were four holes, one hole each side, and it was windy. He stood in the middle of the room, wondering what actually was coming for him.

"I am so enthusiastic to see what is coming for me, I love surprises, and it's so much fun," he said.

There were a lot of noises from these four holes, his position was now guarded, waiting and being very patient. Then came the Servants crawling out of the holes, he slayed as many as he could, and Servants keep coming out the holes.

"Oh, man! What is keeping them coming? How come there are so many? Damn it," he said. He continued killing them, even numerous at once. He was worn out, falling on his knees down on the ground, panting and sighing).

"What the hell? More and more are coming out. They are going to choke me, are they?" he said. He was thinking hard what to do, until the bright light came out of the sword. He turned his head to it and stood up, picking up the sword. He hold sword up in the air, the light blinking and brighter. The wind grow into a vortex, Jeff was in its eye. Servants were pulled into the vortex, and for next few minutes, the vortex continuing. All Servants were pulled into the vortex at once, and decomposed to ashes.

After the vortex completed its task, the Servants were completely gone, not one single cat came out of the holes, nothing. Jeff fell down on the ground again, back into a human form. His power was extinguished. There was nothing left for him. He panted and groaned, he fainted, bumped into the ground and lay there.

"What's taking so long? It has been a few hours now, something's wrong," she said.

"I can feel something's wrong there, we have to go inside, one way or another," he said.

They climbed down the hole into the cave, "Damn it stinks, and it's so dark down there. Once we land there, we need to find something to light up as torches," he said.

"There are plenty of torches down there, I have seen them. Don't worry; let's hurry and get down there, please," she said. Down they went, standing together so closely. Luckily, Timothy had a lighter; he lit it and held the lighter. They walked searching for the torches, eventually, they found three. They only needed two as far as they were concerned.

They found three tunnels just right there. They were not sure which one to take and to look at. The winds came out of the second tunnel suddenly stopping without warning. It gave both of them the idea that Jeff might be there. They lit the torches, one holding each one. They held their hands and sneaked into the tunnel. It was a long tunnel, they continued walking. A little while later, they finally arrived, and entered the room.

"Oh, my god. There are bodies of Servants, even a lot of ashes around here. Let's look for Jeff, shall we?" Timothy said.

They kept looking around, it was very dark, it was difficult for them. Timothy accidentally tripped and fell on the ground. He groaned. "Oh, boy. Damn," he said. He picked up the torch and moved it and saw Jeff was lying down. He waved the torch to get Julianne's attention. "I found Jeff, you better come here, he is sort of injured, I think," he said.

"Not again, damn it, Jeff, I am taking you out of this place right now," she said.

"Remember what Jeff has told you, you can't. Just take him out to the big room where we came in before," he said. Julianne picked him up and carried him with caution. They got back into the tunnel.

When they made it to the area, she put him down on the ground, and held him. She tried many ways to wake him up.

They were waiting and waiting for Jeff to respond. Timothy sat next to him, she held him but not securely enough. Suddenly, Jeff was pulled so quickly, she grabbed his hand and tried to pull him back. She failed, and lost his hands. "Where is he? Where are they taking him?" She was panicking. "I think it's the last tunnel, the third one on the right side. Let's go and get him out of here before it's too late," he said.

# Chapter 18

## The Servant's Nest

Jeff remained unconscious, meanwhile he was being pulled in through the tunnel. Julianne and Timothy ran into the tunnel in a hurry, without the torches. Julianne couldn't find Timothy, she was trying to grab his hand, and that way she could hold on to it without being lost. Timothy stopped, and she bumped into him without knowing. "Thank God, Now, I can hold his hand," she said to herself. Timothy held her hand tight, but gently. She let him lead her by walking ahead, she following him.

There was a blue light blinking down the tunnel. "Look. There's a blue light coming out of there, we better follow it, we might find him," he said.

"All right, let's hurry; I am afraid of what might happen to him," she said. They made haste, walking into the room. Jeff was found on the floor in the middle of circle.

"It's the chamber room, where Kevin transformed into a black cat in front of me before," he said.

A Servant appeared looking very dangerous, growling repeatedly. It pulled Jeff away from them, and he was hit against the wall, making him unconscious.

"Who are you? What do you want from Jeff? Why do you do this?" she asked.

"I had his father killed, and now I am going to kill him, I am going to make you watch it, till his death," it said.

"Oh, God. Please do not kill him; he has done nothing to you, has he? He's only a kid," she said.

"Well, well, I am not going to let him go, nothing can make me. I am going to kill him whether you like it or not," he said. "Who will be first? For me to kill? You? Or you?" he said.

"Let them go, you can take me, for all I care," Timothy said.

"Oooh, what guts, nah, I am not going to do you, I would prefer her," he said.

"Please don't, I am not asking, I am telling you, take me, no matter what you say." he said. Growling, he took his sword out and attempted to attack her. Jeff stood in front of the Servant, while he stood the Servant didn't realize. He continued his attack, but the sword was stopped. The Servant was puzzled, he looked down, Jeff transformed into a black cat in a flash, he had his sword blocking the Servant's attack.

He growled loudly, making a very strong attack with his two swords so purely. "Hey, you two, get out here now. It will not do you good if you stay here. Get out!" Jeff said. "Wait! Wait!" she said, being interrupted, "Shut up! Get out now!" Jeff said. They hastily ran out of the chamber and into the tunnel. They got to the spot where they came in, they climbed back the way they came in, and succeeded in getting out of the cave.

The servant and Jeff continued their battle, very violently, more than any other battles he had been to. "What makes you think you are stronger than I am? You don't have power like I do," it said.

"You have no idea; let's see what I am made of. You yammer too much," Jeff said.

"Take your best shot! I would love to see that." he said. "I guess I am not the only one who talks too much, am I?" it said.

Jeff smiled, his eyes became a greenish glow. His sword turned into a blue light. There was a soul standing right where Jeff stood. "What the hell are you? What are you trying to do?" it asked.

"You will find out, like I said, you have no idea, didn't I?" he said and smiled. He smiled at the Servant, and faded away. The Servant startled himself in confusion, looking for him. "Where are you? Show me yourself? Are you such a coward?" it said. Jeff reappeared behind its back, and slashed its back, then faded away again. Screaming, it turned the Servant into a very pure rage. He heard laughing everywhere.

The soul reappeared inside him, it showed itself. It was Kevin's soul. The Servant was so utterly shocked. "You are supposed to be dead, damn you, Kevin," it said.

"You are finished. You are going back to where you belong," he said.

"No you can't send me back, you aren't as powerful as I am," it said. Kevin dissolved into a fog, a blue one and flew through the Servant's body. It went through its body and attacked repeatedly by going out and in its body. Jeff reappeared and slashed his sword through the Servant's heart.

There was a scream as the Servant turned into ash slowly, and the ashes flew into the air and faded away. Jeff took the sword out, and held it. "Jeff, get out, this cave is about to collapse again," Kevin said.

"Wait! What are you doing here? How did you know I was here?" Jeff asked.

"I will be always here or anywhere you are. My soul is already trapped inside you. Listen to me this time, go, and get out while you can," he said.

"Okay, just one more thing, is it over? Is everything over?" he asked.

"There is nothing that can be just over, it's a long shot. You will see more of the truth in the future. Goodbye," Kevin said. He disappeared.

Julianne and Timothy were waiting outside, starting to feel the earthquake. "What the hell's going on? Are we having an earthquake? Are we?" Timothy asked.

"I have absolutely no idea, it might from the battle down there? We cant go in there, you never know, it will collapse and we will end up stuck down there," she said. Jeff stood alone and said, "Thank you for being here for me when I needed you, Dad." The ceiling beginning to crack and cave in. Jeff turned into a black cat once again.

# Chapter 19

## Demolished

Once Jeff turned into the form of a black cat, The Cave beginning to demolish itself. Jeff started running like a real black cat, in a fast speed. He bounced repeatedly on cave walls to make it faster. He entered the dungeon hall, the chamber had been caved in, rocks were all over there.

"Whoa. Big earthquake, the cave is about to collapse worse than last time," Timothy said.

"Hurry, Jeff, you've got to get out of here," she thought. Jeff succeeded in getting out of the dungeon, into the room where he came in. All three dungeons halls were caved in. "Whew! I got here in time. Damn," he said.

Timothy suddenly got in the car, and drove in reverse for a few blocks away from the collapsed cave. Jeff jumped and flew out of the hole, landing on the ground. He transformed back into the human form while he was walking. He stopped walking, and stood toward his mother and Timothy a few blocks away, and he smiled. "It's over, it's done for," he said.

Somehow, the ground cracked into pieces, Jeff fell down. Julianne ran and grabbed his arm, and pulled him out. He was injured and bleeding. She grabbed him, and carried him in her arms, and took him to the car by running in a panic.

"Hurry up before more cracks appear in the ground," Timothy said. Jeff blacked out, and was non-responsive. He had his mother worrying way too much.

They got in the car, Timothy was driving in a rush, apparently to get on the roads. They were on their way to the hospital. "Wake up! Jeff, Wake up!" She patted his cheek. "Hurry, we gotta get to hospital, his bleeding won't stop," she said. She cried, and sobbed.

"Take it easy. Put pressure on it," he said. Jeff had a bad cut on his shoulder. "We will be there soon, we are almost there," he said.

"He turned back into a black cat again, then back to human form rapidly. What's happening?" she said. Timothy looked at him, he was able to see what was actually happening. It confused him, from what was going on with Jeff. Jeff was remaining unconscious, unresponsive. "Please don't die on me, just don't," she cried loudly and screamed. "I hope this is over with. Since the cave has been so completely desolated, they just went, right?" she asked.

"I am not so sure about that. If it was over, something would have been changed all of a sudden, but it has not yet," he said. "Yeah, let's wait and see, and we will know what has happened, let's focus on Jeff right now," she said.

They arrived at the hospital; Timothy took Jeff and carried him to the emergency room. Julianne held and pressured the wound. Julianne screamed for help, to get a nurse's attention. Several nurses came to them and took Jeff to the hospice bed, ripping his clothes off. Jeff had not moved an inch, nothing.

The nurses cleaned up the wounds, and did other medical procedures to save this boy's life. Julianne and Timothy were ordered to remain in the waiting room. Timothy held her with his arms around her, to comfort her. Julianne was very tired, and was not feeling well.

The doctor appeared and waved at Timothy, Julianne was asleep on his lap. Timothy woke her up, "The doctor is here. Let's see what he has to say, shall we?" he said.

"Your son, Jeff, is resting now; he is in a stable condition right now. We did everything we could to save this boy's life, he is very lucky," he said.

"What do you mean he is lucky?" Timothy said.

"He lost a lot of blood; he could have died from it. We were able to stop the bleeding, we sewed him up well. And we are feeding him some medicines, and other things to keep him in shape, and to heal the wounds," he said. "We would like to keep him in observation for 24 hours since he is in a critical condition, and why don't you guys go home and get some rest, and you guys can come back tomorrow morning to see him," he said.

"Yeah, that would be a good idea, I will take her home and stay with her until later," Timothy said.

Julianne sobbed; she was scared of what might happen to him. "I don't know what to do right now," she said. "Let him rest, we'll get home and get some rest, it might do us all some good one," he said. They walked out and left the hospital to go back home. They drove home, Julianne slept on the mattress instead of the couch and Timothy took the couch instead.

A few days later, Jeff still showed no response. It not only concerned Julianne, but the doctor as well. It had Julianne very worried. "Can't we do something about him? How long will this continue?" she asked.

"We cannot say because there were no changes, we intend to keep him here a little while," he said.

Julianne sobbed lightly. She left to head back home, worrying, being positive about her son. She saw Timothy cooking dinner. "What are you doing? Are you cooking something?" she asked.

"Yes, we have not eaten much the past few days; I bet we are starving to eat a good meal, aren't we?" he said.

"Yeah, that would be great, thanks," she said.

Jeff began to open his eyes a little bit. His eyes were rolling up, he was still in pain. The nurse found him stable, and she contacted the doctor. The doctor rushed to get there to see him. He gave Julianne a call.

"We better get to the hospital, Jeff has made some progress, he is awake now," she said. Timothy and she jumped into the car, and drove off to the hospital excitedly.

# Chapter 20

## Then: Is It Over? Or Not?

Timothy and Julianne arrived at the hospital, make it to the elevator, and taking it up a few floors. Julianne ran into the hallway and entered Jeff's room. Jeff smiled when he saw his mother come in.

"How are you feeling? How is your head?" she asked. "My head is okay, for now," he said.

"Hey, chump. How are you doing? Had fun?" Timothy asked. "Ha. Well, I am fine, at least I am safe right now, from everything, and you know," he said.

"Yes, I got it clear as crystal. Hush-Hush," he said.

"You punk," Jeff said.

"Me? A punk? Nah. You a poopie punk," he said.

"Cut it out, you guys!" she said. "Let him be, he needs some rest, dummy," she said.

"I ain't a dummy, but you? A dummy-doll?" he laughed. Julianne punched and pinched Timothy's arm silly.

"Jeff, listen, have you had any disturbing nightmares lately?" she asked. "No, not yet, I hope it does not come to it again," Jeff sighed.

A doctor came in, and asked for Julianne, "Can I have a moment with you? The interpreter is here," he asked.

"Sure, is everything all right?" she said.

"Yes, I think he will be fine, but I am concerned about him having anemia," he said.

"Oh God, how long will it last?" she asked.

"We don't know for sure yet, we still need to test a bit more, so that way we will get the better results, is that alright with you?" he said.

"Excuse me, I have to go to the vending room, to get something to drink and eat, I need something sweet." Timothy said.

"Get me a Pepsi, will you?" she asked.

"Should I get something for Jeff?" he asked.

"Yes you can, but not too much sugar," the doctor said.

"Okay, I will be right back, it will be a few minutes. Thanks," he said.

Timothy walked and took the stairs to get to the vending room. He felt something bother him, he continued his walk. He had nausea, and felt so weak, and he fell down on the floor hard, he blacked out.

"What's taking him so long? Is he all right?" Julianne thought.

"I better go check on other patients; you go ahead and stay with Jeff. I will be back whenever I have chance, ok?" the Doctor said.

She walked down to the front desk, "What kind of tests does the doctor plan to take on Jeff today?" she asked.

"The doctor wants to give him some sedatives, so he could do a CAT scan, to make sure things are all right," the nurse said.

"Oh, anything else should I know?" she asked again.

"You will know more tests after the CAT scan has been taken. I am sure everything is fine with Jeff. Don't worry too much until further, all right?" the nurse said.

"Okay, I will try my best not to worry over the limit, but thanks," she said. She was on her way to Jeff's room, something stopped her from walking. She felt chills, she looked around at the front desk, and screamed. There was a black cat on the counter walking toward her, "Oh my God. They came back for Jeff, didn't they?" she said.

There were sounds of bangs, smashes, screams. Jeff gasped, he could hear a loud noise. Jeff got up and sat up on the hospice bed. He was quiet and waiting for his mother to come back. Julianne walked backward to the entrance to Jeff's room. The door was now shut loudly, and locked itself. Jeff sobbed, scared, he remained quiet, without any sounds.

The rotten odor spread into his room. He sniffed, shuddering in a scared way. He turned his head around real slow. The servant jumped on Julianne, she screamed. As Jeff turned his head around toward where the window was. He did not know what was happening, or what was going on. He screamed, a Servant there shrieked and growled angrily.

# Epilogue

After the incident at the hospital, a decomposing servant jumped toward Jeff. Timothy put in some coins to get some snacks and drinks. He turned around to the exit, there were numerous servants blocking the door and he was unable to exit. He was shaking and sweating.

Julianne banged the door, the door was locked. She feared for her son, Jeff. The nurses and doctors, everyone including patients went out of control and screamed, running around panicking. Even more servants were coming into the windows in his room. He screamed painfully, inside him he was very burned, like a flame could melt the skins.

He was short of breath, sweating, and was weak enough not to get up. He was currently lying down on the floor. Julianne looked around to find something useful to bash into the door to save him. The servants chased her off, and jumped on her. She was trying to get servants off her.

Again, Jeff fainted and become non-responsive. More servants came into the room, it was getting crowded and suffocating him. Surprisingly, the servants in the room calmed down, and sat quietly and watched him like a hawk.

A few servants walked into the vending room, growling nastily, they looked bloodier than before. He put himself down on the floor and sat in the corner of the vending room. He turned into a 'stircrazy'. Jeff's body began to shake, his eye blinking and glowing greenish, a little more every time they blinked.

"What am I going to do? How can I get over them to get back to her?" Timothy said. Julianne saw an ax hanging with a water hose on the wall near the stair door. She went for it, continuing her fight with servants.

Several patients and nurses had been killed and were eaten by Servants. Some succeeded in staying alive by defending themselves. As for the doctors, most of them were dead and had already been eaten. Nothing out there can be very helpful at the moment.

Julianne acquired an ax, then she went for the window to see if there were any way she could use it to get out. As she approached the window, she said, "Oh, my God. There are flows of servants out there. They are climbing up the building."

Julianne and Timothy were thinking the same phrase: "What are we going to do? Hopefully, Jeff has the strength enough to end all of this."

# Darkness of the Black
## Curse of the Darkness

# Coming Soon

# About the Author

Sean McNulty (A.K.A. Shane Hoover), a first time author. He is profoundly deaf, he was born in New Jersey. His family moved to Delaware for a short time, and they settled in Elkton, Maryland. He was raised there all of his life. He attended Maryland School for the Deaf and graduated at Delaware School for the Deaf. He currently resides in Colorado. He is father of two children. He is looking forward to writing more books in the future.

Autograph

www.ingramcontent.com/pod-product-compliance
Lightning Source LLC
Chambersburg PA
CBHW030532020726
47494CB00004B/1323